Ronald Reagan

Young Leader

Illustrated by Meryl Henderson

Ronald Reagan

Young Leader

by Montrew Dunham

ALADDIN PAPERBACKS

For Griffin, Graham, Robert Davis,
Lauren, Sara, and Mackenzie

First Aladdin Paperbacks edition September 1999

Text copyright © 1999 by Montrew Dunham
Illustrations copyright © 1999 by Meryl Henderson

Aladdin Paperbacks
An imprint of Simon & Schuster Children's Publishing Division
1230 Avenue of the Americas
New York, NY 10020

Printed and bound in the United States of America
4 6 8 10 9 7 5

Library of Congress Catalog Card Number: 99-65082
ISBN 0-689-83006-8

4

Illustrations

Contents

Other COFA by Montrew Dunham:

THURGOOD MARSHALL: YOUNG JUSTICE
JOHN MUIR: YOUNG NATURALIST
ROBERTO CLEMENTE: YOUNG BALL PLAYER
NEIL ARMSTRONG: YOUNG FLIER
ABNER DOUBLEDAY: YOUNG BASEBALL PIONEER
LANGSTON HUGHES: YOUNG BLACK POET
MARGARET BOURKE-WHITE: YOUNG PHOTOGRAPHER
MAHALIA JACKSON: YOUNG GOSPEL SINGER
OLIVER WENDELL HOLMES: BOY OF JUSTICE
GEORGE WESTINGHOUSE: YOUNG INVENTOR
ANNE BRADSTREET: YOUNG PURITAN POET

Ronald Reagan

Young Leader

Chapter One

White fluffy snow lay thick on the ground. Young Ronald was running so fast that he gasped as he caught his breath in the cold, crisp air. He looked back over his shoulder to see his older brother, Neil, catching up to him, so he quickly turned to the right and skidded to a stop at the base of the tall stone monument in the center of the park. Neil went running right past him and when he realized that Ronald had ducked back out of sight, he stopped and whirled around. He stooped quickly and gathered up a handful of the snow and tossed it at his brother.

"Hey, Dutch! I caught you!" Neil shouted to his brother.

"No, you didn't! I got away from you!" Ronald retorted. "I'm safe . . . this monument is a safe place!"

"Since when!"

Chuck and some of the other boys came running up and soon they were all throwing balls of the soft fresh snow at each other. Neil shouted, "Dutch says he's safe here by the monument."

"That's the rule!" Chuck answered. Then he looked puzzled as he asked, "How come you always call him Dutch?"

Neil shook his head. He didn't have time to explain. Impatiently he said, "Our dad started calling him Dutch when he was born . . . and now everybody calls him Dutch."

Suddenly Dutch darted out from behind the base of the monument and started running. And the chase began all over again, with all the boys playing fox-and-geese as they ran through the deep snow in Railroad Park.

Ronald Reagan lived in a pleasant white frame house right by Railroad Park with his father, Jack Reagan, and his mother, Nelle Reagan, and his brother, Neil. The boys loved to play in the park with their friends in summer and in winter. In the center of the park was a tall statue with the figure of a Union soldier on top in honor of the soldiers who had fought in the Civil War and in the Spanish-American War. There was also a large iron cannon from the Civil War with a pyramid of big cannonballs stacked beside it. Alongside the park on Main Street were the railroad tracks, and the railroad station was just beyond that.

The Reagan family had moved to the house by the park when Ronald was just three months old. He was born on a cold, snowy day, February 6, 1911, in an apartment over a bakery on Main Street in Tampico, a very small town set in the middle of fertile Illinois farmland. This was the same apartment where his brother, Neil, had been born two years earlier. Main Street was lined with the stores where the nearby farmers came to shop, and often the street was lined with the horse and wagons they had driven to town. Most of the stores had apartments on the second floor of the buildings and many of the shopkeepers lived in the apartments over their stores. Jack Reagan, Ronald's father, worked in the Pitney General Store, which was across the street from the apartment where they had lived.

On this December day when the boys were playing fox-and-geese, the park was blanketed with snow, which had blown into uneven mounds making glimmering hills and valleys of sparkling white drifts. Dutch ran through the snow leaving his footprints, and Neil and Chuck ran after him following in his tracks. When Dutch came to the edge of the park, he slid to a stop and pointed at the locomotive, which was pulling out of the station.

"Look, the train's leaving!" he shouted excitedly.

The boys all gathered around to watch the train pull out. They never knew exactly when the train would arrive or when it would leave. The Hooppole, Yorktown, and Tampico Railroad had only one train. It departed from the village of Hooppole between 8:30 and 10:00 in the morning to come the fourteen miles to Tampico. Along the way it would stop at places like Aliceville and Love Center.

The train was made up of the locomotive, two boxcars for freight, and a bright red caboose. If there were any passengers they would ride in the caboose. The little train left

Tampico to return to Hooppole anytime between 3:30 P.M. and 7:00 P.M. The train would leave whenever the freight was loaded into the boxcars and the passengers were ready to go.

It was exciting for the boys to watch the train. The big black locomotive was belching steam and black smoke into the cold air, looking as if it were almost alive as it pulsed with the sound of the steam. Slowly as it gathered steam, the huge driver wheels started to move and pulled the train out of the station. The locomotive huffed and puffed rhythmically as it gained speed and clicked down the track going out of town.

As the train rolled out of sight, Dutch ran over to the mound of cannonballs. He crouched behind them and gathered up loose snow to form it into a snowball. It was hard to make a nice round snowball with his heavy mittens.

Neil ran behind the statue, and Chuck

scurried behind a tree. The other boys came running and soon the air was filled with laughter and shouting as they pelted one another with their snowballs.

Dutch threw three or four more snowballs in rapid succession, and then he ran to the cannon where he clambered up to sit astride the top. When he got on top, he threw his hands up into the air triumphantly and shouted, "Look at me!"

Suddenly he lost his balance on the slippery snow and fell to the ground! The boys all gathered around, "Are you all right?"

Dutch couldn't answer at first, he was so dazed from his fall. But soon he sat up, shook his head, and said, "For a moment I thought I was in heaven!"

As he scrambled to his feet, Neil said, "Let's go in. I'm hungry!" And so Dutch and Neil ran into the house where their mother was in the kitchen cooking and baking. The shelf on the cupboard was lined with freshly baked pies, and Nelle was just taking Christmas cookies out of the stove. Everything smelled so good!

Neil started to take a cookie from the cookie sheet as Mother stopped him. "You can have one as soon as they cool a little."

Neil pulled his hand back and immediately asked his mother, "How long until Christmas?"

Mother laughed as she put another sheet of cookies into the oven to bake, "It's still a few days away."

"How many days?" Dutch pressed for an answer as he unwrapped his snow-covered scarf from his neck.

Mother stepped back as the bits of snow flew off the scarf and said quickly, "Both of you get your snowy, wet coats off and hang them on the hook with your caps and scarves."

"But how many . . . " Neil persisted.

Nelle Reagan sat down at the table,

thought a moment, and then answered, "I guess it's four days until Christmas Day."

"And that's when Santa Claus will bring our electric train," Neil said confidently.

"Are Aunt Jennie and our cousins coming then?" Dutch asked.

Mother answered Dutch patiently, "Yes, Aunt Jennie and her whole family will be here for Christmas." She didn't say anything about the electric train.

But Neil continued, "And we can all play with the electric train!"

Then Dutch added his question, "Will our train be just like the one at the station?"

Mother took a deep breath as she put her elbow on the table and rested her chin on her hand. She knew she had to say something. The boys were so set on getting the electric train, and she didn't want them to be disappointed.

Gently she said, "I'm not sure that Santa Claus has any electric trains this year."

Each day Nelle had said that she didn't think Santa had any electric trains. She tried to let the boys know they probably wouldn't get a train. Jack Reagan worked hard as a salesman at the Pitney General Store in Tampico to support his family, but toy trains cost more than they could really afford.

The days went so slowly. Dutch and Neil thought that Christmas would never come! Every day Neil asked about their electric train and every day their mother would explain patiently that they should not expect Santa to bring an electric train.

Each evening they sat around the table while Mother read a story to them. On Christmas Eve the boys were so excited they could hardly pay attention to the story. Mother took them up to bed and tucked them in. Her auburn hair gleamed in the lamplight, and her eyes looked so blue as she leaned down to kiss each of them good night.

Dutch snuggled down into bed as his mother gave him one last hug.

Dutch closed his eyes tightly and tried to go to sleep, but he couldn't. He wanted to go to sleep, so that the night would pass and he could wake up on Christmas morning. He twisted and turned and finally whispered, "Neil, are you asleep?"

Neil sat up in bed and whispered back, "Listen, I think I hear something."

Dutch had the covers up over his head and he pulled them down to listen. "What? I don't hear anything . . . "

"Shh . . . just listen!"

Dutch sat up and listened more carefully. He could hear a kind of whirring. . . . "Do you mean that buzzing sound?"

Neil nodded. Then they also heard some laughter along with the whirring sounds. Softly Neil said, "Come on."

As he crawled out of bed, Dutch threw the covers back and swung his feet out on

the cold floor. The two boys crept very quietly to the top of the staircase and listened. The whirring sounds grew louder with regular metallic clicks every now and then. Then there was laughter! Step by step they crept down the stairs to peek through the banister into the parlor. As Neil grinned and pointed, Dutch saw his father and mother on the floor by the Christmas tree. A little electric train was whirling about the train track. Mother had her hand up to her face as she laughed with pleasure, and their father was chuckling as he was pushing the handle on the control, which made the train go around.

Dutch said, "Look, there's a locomotive, a box car . . . and a little red caboose . . . just like the real train!"

Neil shushed Dutch and punched him to go back on upstairs, so they wouldn't be heard. They ran upstairs and hopped into bed. Dutch persisted, "but did you see the little red caboose!"

Neil laughed as he answered, "Yes, a red caboose!"

They never told their parents that they had seen their Christmas surprise on Christmas Eve!

Chapter Two

Dutch was suddenly awake, and though it was still dark outside, he knew it was Christmas morning! He had a happy memory of the electric train, but he almost felt as if it weren't real. He wondered if he had dreamed about seeing the train last night.

"Neil! Neil!" he called as he pounded his brother on his shoulder. "Wake up, it's Christmas morning!"

"I'm awake! Neil shouted as he popped out of bed and onto his feet. "I'm awake! Come on . . . let's go downstairs!"

The two boys ran down the stairs as fast as they could, and when they saw the electric train with its locomotive standing on the train track around the Christmas tree, they both shouted with glee! Their mother and father watched with pleasure at their delight! Dutch ran over to lie down on the floor by the train. He touched the locomotive, the boxcar, and the little red caboose. He exclaimed, "It has a red caboose . . . just like the real train!"

"All freight trains have to have a caboose," his father explained. "That's always the last car of the train, even when there are many boxcars. It's where the train crew rides."

Neil ran straight to the transformer to turn on the train and make it run. "My turn!" he shouted as he pushed the switch and the little train chugged right around the track. And then after that the boys took turns running the train.

Christmas Day was such a blur of happiness!

Aunt Jennie, Mother's sister, and her family came through the heavy snow by bobsled drawn by a team of two horses. The house was filled with laughter and talking. The children played with the electric train and the Christmas toys the cousins had brought with them all. And then after Christmas dinner, they bundled up in their heavy coats and scarves and ran outside to play in the snow in the park.

After Christmas, the days settled into regular living. Tampico was a very pleasant small town. The boys played in the park with their friends, their father worked at the Pitney General Store, and their mother took care of them. On Sundays, Mother and Dutch went to church at the Tampico Church of Christ and Father and Neil usually went to mass at St. Mary's Catholic Church. Since Jack Reagan was Catholic, when Neil was born he was baptized in the Catholic Church, but when Ronald was born Nelle decided that he would go to her church. Nelle spent a lot of time with activities in her church, and she was always very kind and helpful to people who were sick or were in trouble.

Suddenly their lives changed! Jack Reagan told Nelle that the J. C. Pitney General Store was sold and that he would have to find another job. The job he found was as a shoe salesman at the very large Fair Store in Chicago, and the family moved to Chicago!

They moved to an apartment on the South Side, not too far from the University of Chicago. Neil and Dutch were lonely in the small apartment. They could play with their electric train, but they couldn't go outside by themselves to the park to play with their friends as they always had. Neil said he wished they could go out to play like they used to in Tampico.

Nelle said, "Just be glad you have your electric train and your toys to play with inside where it is nice and warm, and we can always read." Their mother read to them every day and oftentimes she would tell them interesting stories as she was ironing or cooking.

Nelle was very thrifty. She would make a large kettle of soup for the family and make it last for several days. On Saturdays, when she went to the butcher, she would ask for liver for the cat, even though they didn't have a cat. The butcher would give her the liver without charge, because not many people liked to eat liver. She would cook it with a little bacon and onions for Sunday dinner.

Although the family did not have much money, Nelle felt it was important to share with people who had less than they did. She continued to take food to people who were hungry or sick. Nelle visited older people who were lonely, and she would read to them. Through her church she was always helping other people.

One afternoon Mother ladled some of her

good hot soup into a large bowl, and covered it carefully with a nice clean tea towel to take to a sick lady who lived in the neighborhood.

Neil and Dutch were playing with their toys on the floor when she left. "I am just going to take this soup to Mrs. Long, who is sick in bed," Nelle told them. "She is so very sick. I may read the Bible to her as well, but I won't be gone very long."

The boys played with their train and some other toys, but after a while they grew tired of their play. "I wish we could go outside," Neil complained.

As it grew late, the apartment grew darker and darker. The apartment was lit by one single gas jet, which Nelle had left burning. Dutch looked out the front window and said, "It's getting dark. I wonder where Mother is."

"Maybe she's lost," Neil replied. "Maybe we should go find her!"

The flame in the gaslight on the wall flickered, and long gray shadows darted back and forth across the room. The darkness was frightening. Dutch looked all around him. "Maybe Dad will be home soon," he paused for a moment, "then he can find Mother."

Neil shook his head. "Dad is at work downtown at the store. He won't be home for a long time. I think we had better find Mother."

Dutch hesitated. "Where will we look?"

"We will just look around, and we can ask people if they know where she is. . . ." Neil looked at the gaslight. "But we had better blow out the light before we go." And so he blew out the flame, but he didn't know that he should also turn off the gas!

The boys wandered up and down the busy city streets. There were so many people, but they didn't see their mother, nor anyone they knew! The boys looked everywhere as they stared at all the people. As they walked along they saw carriages, wagons, trolley cars, and automobiles. Everything and everybody seemed to be in a hurry. There were the bustling noises of the demanding bells of the trolley cars, the hoofbeats of horses, and the bleating horns of automobiles!

Suddenly a pair of horses raced down the middle of the street pulling a huge red fire engine with its bell clanging and steam rising behind it! Dutch stepped back against a building as the fire engine went roaring past! He looked at the firemen in their black coats and black fire hats hanging on to the fire truck as it raced along. He wondered how they could hang on as the fire engine swerved and turned to miss carriages and wagons along the street.

Dutch was still looking after the fire engine, and thinking how exciting it would be to be a fireman and ride on a fire truck, when a strange man came up to him. The man staggered and his dark eyes looked wild. Neil stepped back a little, but the man leaned down and said, "What are you two boys doing out here alone!"

In the meantime Nelle had returned to the apartment, and when she went in she could smell the escaping gas! Quickly she covered her nose and mouth and ran to turn off the gas jet. She called and called for the boys! She was terrified! She could not imagine what had happened to them. She ran out the open door and down the street where she saw the strange-looking man talking to Neil and Dutch. She ran to the boys and gathered them into her arms as she shouted at them, "What are you boys doing?"

"Lady, I was just telling these two that they needed to be going home," growled the man unpleasantly.

"You are quite right," Nelle said crisply. "Come, both of you!" And she grabbed them by their hands and marched them back to the apartment.

Neil and Dutch never forgot how angry their parents were and the paddling Jack gave them while Nelle watched.

* * *

They lived in Chicago for a short time until Jack got a job at O. T. Johnson's Department Store in Galesburg, a rather small town in western Illinois almost 200 miles from Chicago. Dutch and Neil were so glad when they moved to Galesburg where there were big green trees and open fields. It was great to be able to play outside and roam again.

They moved into a nice big house, which even had an attic. Soon after they moved in, Dutch went up to the attic to explore. Carefully he walked under the rafters as he looked at the stacks of boxes. When he looked to see what they were, he found case after case containing a large collection of beautiful, delicate butterflies and colorful bird eggs. He felt as rich as if he had discovered a treasure! One by one he would take the glass cases out and with his nose close to the case, study all the details on the fragile wings of the butterflies. There were many cases of colorful bird eggs, and he marveled at the many different sizes and colors of the eggs. He spent hours in the attic admiring these wonders.

Neil and Dutch went to school in Galesburg. Neil was in third grade and Dutch started school in the first grade, although he could already read. On April 6, 1917, the United States entered World War I. Jack Reagan tried to enlist in the army, but he wasn't taken because he had two young sons.

Nelle took Neil and Dutch down to the train station to watch the soldiers coming through on troop trains. There were Red Cross ladies handing out doughnuts to the soldiers. The young men in their khaki uniforms would lean out the windows to wave at all the people who had come down to the station to wish them well. Nelle gave Dutch a penny and held him up so that he could give the penny for good luck to one of the soldiers. As the train pulled out of the station, Nelle, Neil, and Dutch stood on the platform and waved until it was completely out of sight.

When Dutch was in second grade the family moved again, this time from Galesburg to Monmouth, where Jack got a job as a shoe salesman at the E. B. Colwell Department Store. Monmouth was the fourth town in which the Reagan family had lived, in just seven years!

Chapter Three

Dutch took a deep breath as he walked up the long flight of steps to the new school in Monmouth. When he walked in with some other boys and girls, no one paid any attention to him. It was always hard for him to have to go to a new school where he didn't know anyone, but this time it was harder than ever.

He hesitated as he got to the door and looked back at the small, treeless playground and then up at the formidable four-story brick building. He sighed deeply as he walked into the wide corridor.

He soon found his classroom, and he felt a little better when the third grade teacher, Miss Luhens, welcomed him to her class. One of the girls, Laura Hays, introduced him to the class, though no one else in the class was very friendly. He sat very stiffly at his desk and he was glad when the day was over and he could run home.

Neil ran into the house ahead of Dutch and shouted, "I'm going out to play with some of the guys."

Dejectedly, Dutch sat down at the kitchen table. Nelle poured a glass of milk and put it on the table in front of him. She looked at him carefully and asked gently, "Is there something wrong?" She always seemed to know how Dutch felt.

Dutch looked at his mother. It helped that she always seemed to understand. He said slowly, "I don't like school . . . the kids . . ."

"Aren't friendly?" Nelle finished his sentence.

Dutch nodded.

"It will take a little time, Dutch. Just be your own friendly self and you will make friends," Nelle tried to encourage him.

Dutch tried to believe that, but it only got worse. Miss Luhens would ask him questions if some of the other pupils did not know the answer. She was very impressed at how fast Dutch could solve problems in multiplication and division. While Laura Hays was always nice to him, the other kids seemed really angry when he could answer questions that they couldn't.

When school was out he just walked home with his shoulders back and his head held high with a special air about him as if he didn't care. Some of the bigger kids would try to chase him and he tried not to pay any attention. There was one bully who followed him day after day trying to beat him up.

One day as he was nearly home, the bully came after him, and he ran to the porch where his mother was standing. Nelle had her arms folded over her chest, and her face was stern. "Go back and fight that bully!"

Dutch didn't want to, and he started to go up on the porch.

His mother said firmly, "You can't come in until you fight that boy!"

Dutch couldn't believe that his calm, gentle mother would make him get into a fight! Filled with fright, he ran down to the bully with his arms swinging. To his surprise, after he had landed a couple of punches, the bigger boy took off and ran. And he never bullied Dutch again! Dutch had learned a valuable lesson in not running away.

Finally school was out for the summer, and by the end of school some of the kids in his class were becoming friendlier. Dutch loved the outdoors and being able to run and play. He often thought about the collections in the attic in the house where they used to live in Galesburg, and he decided he would like to collect his own butterflies and birds' eggs.

He would go out in the woods and walk through the meadows and along the little streams looking for butterflies. Sometimes he would catch some beautiful butterflies and bring them home. Nelle told him how caterpillars would spin a cocoon and then turn into butterflies. This seemed like a miracle to him.

Dutch wanted to collect birds' eggs, too, but Nelle told him, "A mother bird is like a human mother and she knows how many eggs she has in her nest."

Dutch was perplexed. "But how can I find eggs for my collection?"

"You can pick up eggs that have fallen from the nest," Nelle answered. "Sometimes there

are too many eggs in a nest and one will fall on the ground. If the egg is out of the nest too long it won't hatch, so it's all right to collect those eggs. Sometimes you'll find an egg that is empty after the baby bird has hatched."

"But those eggs would be broken!"

"Yes, but sometimes we can put the shell back together . . . and even broken, the eggs can still be beautiful."

Oftentimes the kids played among the stately big trees on the green lawns of the Monmouth College campus. One day as Dutch was running along, he saw a nest that had fallen from a tree. Nearby on the street there were four baby birds that had spilled out when the nest had fallen. They were flopping about with their wings. Their little beaks were wide open as they waited for their mother. They looked so pitiful!

Quickly Dutch scooped up each tiny bird

and gently put it back in the nest. He looked up in the tree and saw a crook in a branch where he thought the nest would fit. Holding the nest carefully in one hand, he climbed up the tree. He placed the nest on the branch securely against the tree trunk where he thought the mother could find it.

Then he slid down the tree trunk. A bird lover, who was looking out his window from his house across the street, had seen what Dutch had done and called out to him, "Good work!"

As Dutch walked home, he thought about what his mother often said, that things always turn out for the best. Summertime was always fun, and when fall came and he started back to school, that was okay too.

And then on November 11, 1918, the armistice was signed, which ended the World War. The war to "end all wars" was over! There was no school, and the entire town turned out to celebrate the victory. This was the most exciting day Dutch had ever experienced!

Neil came running in the house. "Everyone says there's going to be a parade! Can we go!"

"Oh yes, we'll go," Nelle answered quickly as she put on her hat and coat.

Dutch was standing by the door and as they went out they could see all their neighbors coming from their houses and joining in the crowd walking down the street to town.

Everyone was talking and laughing all at the same time. It was like a giant party! When they got down to town, they lined up on the sidewalk to watch as the parade came by. There were bands, and old soldiers, veterans of other wars, and anyone who wanted to march, parading past, as the onlookers cheered and shouted!

Suddenly there were massive thuds and a blaze of fireworks lighting up the sky. Dutch and Neil watched in wonderment as the fireworks went on and on.

"Look," Dutch cried as he saw the light from a large fire down the next street. Nelle and the boys followed the crowd to where there was a great bonfire built in the middle of a street burning a scarecrow effigy of Kaiser Bill, the king of Germany!

The air was chilly, and the short November afternoon had faded into darkness, but no one minded. The parade went on and on with streams of people shouting and crying as they held blazing torches high against the dark sky.

Dutch felt an excitement, but also an inner feeling of sadness for all the strange mysteries of war, and he wondered about those soldiers he had seen on the troop train. Where were they now with all this celebration?

Shortly after this wondrous, explosive celebration, came a sickness, which fell upon the town. Actually all over the country there was an epidemic of influenza, which was taking lives. At this time there were no flu shots to keep people from getting the flu, nor were there any antibiotics to make people well. Everyone started wearing masks, so that they would not spread the disease. As Dutch walked to school he would see houses with a wreath and black ribbon on the door, which meant someone in that house had died of influenza. Dutch asked Miss Luhens, "Does everybody who gets the flu die?"

She shook her head sadly, "Not always, Dutch, but it does seem that many people who get the flu do die."

Each day there were more and more pupils absent from school, because either they or their parents had caught the flu. Finally school was closed, not only because so few students were able to come, but also so that the contagion would not spread.

The principal announced to their class, "School will be temporarily closed to prevent possible contagion. Please take your books home, and try to continue reading and doing your arithmetic. You will be notified when school will open. I hope this terrible flu epidemic will soon be over, and we will all be well and back in school."

But it was not over soon enough. Nelle was stricken with the flu! Dutch would steal to the doorway of her bedroom to look at her. He couldn't believe that she was so sick. Nelle was never sick! She didn't move. She didn't say anything. She just lay motionless in her bed day after day.

Dutch and Neil were so frightened. They didn't know what to do without Nelle. The house was so still and dark. Dutch sat by the window each day to watch for Dr. Laurence to come with his little black bag. He couldn't even think about what would happen if his mother didn't get well. Tears rolled out of his eyes and down his cheeks. He just couldn't imagine what he would do without his mother.

Without saying anything, the doctor went up to see Nelle. When the doctor came down the stairs, Dutch looked carefully at his face but he couldn't tell what the doctor was thinking. The doctor's face was so serious. The doctor said to Jack, "If you can get her to eat, give her as much moldy cheese as she will eat."

"Moldy cheese?" Jack questioned.

The doctor nodded, "Sometimes it helps and it won't do any harm." Then Dr. Laurence took Jack's arm, and nodded toward the boys. "Let's just step outside."

Dutch would almost hold his breath and his stomach would tighten with fear. He was so afraid of what the doctor was going to tell Jack. He looked at his father when he came back into the house. His heart pounded. Jack looked so sad.

Day after day they waited. Finally, one day

when the doctor came, Jack came in with a smile on his face as he said, "She's going to be all right."

Dutch felt like a weight had been lifted from his heart.

Chapter Four

After her terrible bout of influenza Nelle had to stay in bed for a while to rest and regain her strength. Dutch and Neil ran up and down stairs, taking her meals to her until she was strong enough to come downstairs. At first she couldn't do very much, and she needed the boys to help her. Gradually she was able to do more and more.

Then, one evening, Nelle went into the kitchen and started to make the popcorn, to get ready to read just like they always had every night before she got sick. Dutch

ran over to Nelle and hugged her. Now everything was back to the way Mother was before she had gotten sick. Her dark auburn hair was smooth and her blue eyes were so clear and true as she looked at Dutch and smiled.

"Are you all right?" Dutch asked. He knew she looked healthy again but he needed her to tell him.

Nelle poured the hard kernels of popcorn into the hot iron kettle, and turned to answer Dutch. "I am just fine . . . just like I had never been sick. Now go get your brother and tell him the popcorn is almost ready, and we are going to read a story."

Nelle poured the white fluffy popcorn into a bowl, drizzled melted butter over it, sprinkled it with salt, and put it on the table. Neil and Dutch pulled up their chairs to the table and Nelle started to read, just like she always did.

It was a long spring, as the boys went back

to school. They had to study very hard to catch up on all the schoolwork that all the students had missed when the school was closed.

That summer the Reagan family moved yet again! This time they were moving back to Tampico! Mr. H. C. Pitney had offered Jack a job again in the Pitney General Store. They moved into an apartment above the Pitney store, which was across Main Street from the apartment where both of the boys were born.

Nelle and the boys were glad to move back to Tampico, to go back where they had friends. With all their moving from one town to another it hadn't been easy for the boys to make lasting friendships. It seemed they would be in a town just long enough to begin to make friends when they would move again and have to leave their new friends.

The Greenman Jewelry Store was next

door to Pitney's store and Dutch soon made friends with the Greenmans. He loved to go into their parlor, which was very special. There was a unique sweet, spicy fragrance in their parlor and so many things to see. There was a horsehair-stuffed loveseat with ornately carved wooden arms. The sofa had a brilliantly colored silk scarf tossed artfully over the back, and there were lace pieces laid carefully over the arms of the chairs. Sometimes Dutch would sit on the sofa and just look at the birds and flowers on the table under their globes of glass and the stacks of leather-bound books.

The Greenmans were an older couple who had no children. They especially liked Dutch, and asked him to call them Aunt Emma and Uncle Jim. Dutch would stop in to see them almost every day. Uncle Jim would usually be in the store. Dutch looked at the beautiful silver gleaming on the table at the back of the store and the row of many different clocks all along the wall ticking away. Uncle Jim would smile and sometimes he would show Dutch a special gem that he was putting into a ring for a customer. Dutch was always quiet and respectful as he admired Uncle Jim's work.

"Is that Dutch out there?" Aunt Emma called.

Uncle Jim patted Dutch on the back, "I think she has something for you . . . go on in the kitchen. I think I smell cookies.

And of course he smelled cookies! Aunt Emma always had cookies for Dutch, whenever he stopped in, and some hot chocolate to go with the cookies. He sat down at the table, and Aunt Emma sat down to talk with him. She was always interested as he told her about his friends or the book his mother was reading to them. Dutch also liked to listen to her stories about when she was a little girl long ago. Then when Uncle Jim closed the shop for the evening he came in and sat down with Dutch and Aunt Emma and they all talked.

There were so many things to do in Tampico. There was a stockyard where the farmers brought their cattle to be sold. The herds of cattle would lope along the dirt streets, raising dust behind them as they were driven to the stockyard. After they were auctioned off they were loaded onto the box-cars of the train to be taken to the city to market. Sometimes when the auction was going on the boys would sit up on the rail fence and watch.

They liked to watch the train chuffing in and out of the village. And when the ice wagon stopped on Main Street to deliver the big chunks of ice for the iceboxes, the boys would follow along behind and tease the ice man to give them the nice cold slivers of ice to suck. They would run bare-footed down the dusty street following the trickles of water, which dripped from the ice wagon.

The boys loved to go swimming and Dutch was one of the best swimmers of all the boys! He and his friends went out north of town to swim in the little creeks and ditches. And then when they tired of swimming in the shallow water, Dutch said, "Let's go to the canal to swim, where the water is deeper."

The boys walked single file along the railroad cinder path, as Dutch led the way to the deep, dangerous Hennepin Canal. As soon as they were almost there Dutch started to run, and with a short jump into the air, dived into the fresh cool water of the canal. One of the boys dived in after him, but two or three of the others just sat on the bank and dangled their feet in the water. Dutch swam upstream a ways and then he turned around and swam back downstream, then over to the bank of the canal with strong sure strokes. He loved the free feeling of gliding through the water.

Harold "Monkey" Winchell lived right across the street from Dutch in the apartment over the Winchells' family shoe store. He and Dutch were friends, but they each had their own gang of friends. Dutch's friends were the "West Side Alley Gang," and Monkey's friends were the "East Side Alley Gang."

Dutch and his friends would make plans on where they would meet and how they would run to get away from Monkey and his group. When there was not an auction at the stockyards, and there was no one there, Dutch and the West Side Alley Gang would meet and play a game of getting away from Monkey's gang. They raced across the pens of the stockyard, swinging from pen to pen and leaping from gate to gate. As they went through a gate, they slammed it behind them quickly so that Monkey and his friends could not catch up with them.

Dutch sneaked up to the gate and peaked through to see where the East Side Gang was, when he got pelted in the face with a soft, rotten tomato!

Quickly he gathered his friends together, and ran over to a garbage can. They pulled out some rotten fruit and tomatoes, and with this ammunition, they returned fire on Monkey and his friends. The battle went on and on until all the garbage had been thrown at the other side. No one ever got hurt, but after being hit and splashed with rotten tomatoes, all of the boys had to slink back home to wash up before their mothers saw them!

One day after a rotten tomato battle, Dutch ran in the back door, when Aunt Emma called, "Dutch, come in . . . I have some fresh cookies coming out of the oven."

"Oh, I will," he answered hastily, "but I need to wash up first." He didn't want her to see him all covered with mud and tomatoes.

Quickly he ran down to the Greenmans' apartment. He went in through the back door of the store, and then on into Aunt Emma's kitchen. He loved coming to the jewelry shop and their house. Dutch didn't have any grandparents, and Aunt Emma and Uncle Jim were almost like having grandparents of his very own. The Greenmans gave him a weekly allowance of ten cents, and Dutch tried to do helpful tasks or errands for them so they would know he really appreciated it.

When fall came, Dutch and Neil went to school in the white frame two-story building, which had the elementary grades on the first floor and the high school on the second floor. Dutch liked school in Tampico where he was an A student. He did well in all his subjects, and he had an especially good memory for dates and historical events. He was so interested in learning about the explorers, who had come down the waterways into and through Illinois. He also found it amazing to realize that the great President Abraham Lincoln was from Illinois, and so he loved studying about Lincoln's life.

Each evening the Reagans sat around the kitchen table. Nelle would put the big bowl of hot buttered popcorn in the center of the table and sometimes they had apples and salted crackers as well. Jack Reagan sat at the end reading the newspaper, and Nelle read a book to Neil and Dutch while they munched popcorn and listened to the story of King Arthur and the Round Table or the Three Musketeers. It was in Tampico that a pretty little cat came to live with them. She would climb on Nelle's lap, and look as if she were listening to the tales of King Arthur and his court, so they decided she should be called Guinevere.

✿　✿　✿

When Christmas came they took a train to visit their aunt and uncle, who had a farm near Morrison, Illinois. The wind was blowing and huge flakes of snow were dancing and swirling as they got off the train. It was very cold as they stood on the platform looking for their relatives. Dutch was so bundled up that the moisture from his breathing made ice crystals on his wool scarf, which was wrapped tightly over his mouth and around his neck. They stood for only a short time, stamping their feet up and down to keep warm, when their uncle met them with a sleigh!

The team of draft horses stood patiently while Dutch and Neil and their parents climbed into the sleigh. They warmed their feet with the hot bricks and tucked in the buffalo robes over their laps. The sleigh bells jingled as they glided over the deep winter snow.

Dutch loved the adventure! With the

merry sound of the bells and the sound of the horses' hooves on crunchy white snow, it almost seemed like a scene out of a storybook.

One of the high points of the holiday was listening to a crystal radio set. Dutch had never seen anything like it! After dinner one of his cousins brought out the little radio. It was a long cylinder, wound with a copper-looking wire, and mounted on a rather rough board, and a long tail of wire, which his cousin called the antenna.

"What is that long wire for?" Dutch whispered to one of the younger boys.

"That's the wire that receives the radio waves," he answered.

Dutch didn't say anything as he watched the boys set it up. They stretched the antenna wire out and hooked it up over the top of the window. Then they got out the earphones and plugged them in.

"Wait until you hear this," his uncle said as

his cousin moved a little metal clip, which was the tuner, and faintly from the earphones, which he held up, you could hear faraway music.

One of Dutch's cousins had built the little radio, and it was a marvel! The whole family gathered around to take turns listening with the earphones. When Dutch put on the earphones and listened, he was astonished to hear the raspy recorded music. What a wonderful instrument! He could hear faint voices saying, "This is KDKA, Pittsburgh . . . and then the sound went dead.

When he couldn't hear anything more, Dutch stood up in the middle of the room and imitated the announcer. "This is KDKA, Pittsburgh! You are listening to KDKA Pittsburgh!" The room was full of people and they all laughed and applauded Dutch, the announcer! And so he got up and did it all over again.

Chapter Five

That next summer, Jack Reagan was beginning to want to move again. He felt like he was not making enough money working for Mr. Pitney in Tampico. Mr. Pitney made an agreement with Jack that he would give him a job and an opportunity for part ownership in a store he owned in Dixon, if Jack would stay until the store in Tampico was sold.

Jack agreed, but in the meantime he looked around for other ways to make money. He decided he could buy a carload of potatoes at a fair price and then sell the potatoes at a profit and make some money.

He made arrangements to buy the carload of potatoes and he decided to have Neil and Dutch go through the potatoes to sort out the good potatoes from the bad.

"I have a job for you boys," Jack said one day as they all walked down together to the big freight car full of potatoes. Jack explained what they were to do. "You go through the potatoes and sort out the good potatoes from the bad. The good potatoes you put into these bags to sell." He showed them the stacks of bags. "And throw the bad potatoes in the garbage."

"How do we know which are the good potatoes and which are the ones you can't sell?" Dutch asked.

Jack laughed. "You'll know all right! Now climb up into the car."

This turned out to be one of the most unpleasant experiences that Dutch and

Neil ever had! When the boys climbed into the boxcar, they sunk knee deep in squishy, smelly potatoes. The boxcar was hot from the summer sun and stinky from the rotten potatoes.

Neil and Dutch both protested. "I can't stand up," Neil shouted as he listed from side to side as he tried to get his footing in the slimy potatoes.

"And it stinks in here!" Dutch added, laughing.

Jack Reagan stood by the open door and said, "It won't take too long. We need to get the good potatoes so that we can sell them and make a profit." Then he turned and went back to his job at the Pitney General Store and left the boys to sort out the potatoes!

Neil and Dutch looked at each other. Then they sat down and started to pick out the good potatoes. There was no doubt which were the bad potatoes! They were soft, rotten, and smelled awful! Day after day they

sat in the hot boxcar picking out the firm, good potatoes and putting them in bags to be sold. Finally the stack of potatoes was more bad than good and they really had to search to find the good potatoes. Neil looked at Dutch and Dutch looked at Neil. Without saying a word, they started tossing all of the potatoes into the garbage, good or bad! When they had finished, they climbed out of the boxcar and marched off. "I don't care if I never see another potato," declared Dutch.

"Me either!" Neil agreed loudly as he wiped his hands on his pants.

They marched home and told their mother they were finished. She smiled with understanding; she knew what an unpleasant job they had. "You both take baths and clean up, we are going to church."

Nelle Reagan gave dramatic recitals for church events and at social functions. This was an outlet for her dramatic talent and relaxation from her duties as a mother and her charitable work. She recited poetry with great expression and emotion.

"I'm going to the Ladies Aid Society, Dutch, and I want you to recite two of your poems."

Dutch had learned a couple of funny poems, which his mother had taught him. That afternoon his mother gave some of her dramatic readings and then she introduced him.

"Ladies, this afternoon I would like to introduce my son, Ronald Reagan, who will recite two poems for you." Nelle Reagan was full of pride as she introduced Dutch.

Dutch walked to the front of the room, and looked at all the ladies in front of him as they were waiting for his performance. He felt a little anxious, but he knew he could remember all the poems and he even felt a little twinge of excitement. With dramatic flair, he recited the first poem the way his mother had taught him. All the ladies clapped enthusiastically and asked him to do another poem.

He looked at his mother, and she nodded, so he recited the second poem, which was really funny. The ladies all laughed merrily and clapped. Dutch felt so good as he heard them laugh and clap. When he bowed, the ladies clapped even more. The applause as he walked out of the room was music to his ears. He felt so special! They were laughing and applauding for *him*!

Dutch was still feeling that happy glow when he and his mother came back home after the program. Guinevere came running up when they walked in the door and wound around his feet as he went to get his book. He stretched out on the floor to read with his head almost on his book. No one ever noticed how close he was to his books as he read, or that he always managed to sit in one of the front desks at school.

Guinevere loved it when Dutch was on the

floor, and she strolled around his arms and shoulders, rubbing against him so that he had trouble seeing his book. He would pet her and then try to move her aside so that he could read.

Often Guinevere would also crawl in bed with him after he was asleep. One night she lay on his chest and woke him up. Dutch frowned as he awakened, he could hear loud talking in his parents' bedroom. He listened, but he couldn't hear what they were saying. Dutch jabbed Neil with his elbow. "Neil, do you hear Mother and Dad? What's wrong? What are they saying?"

Neil just stirred sleepily and mumbled, "They yell at each other sometimes."

Dutch didn't understand. He'd never heard his mother raise her voice! Dutch got out of bed. His mother heard him and came into the boys' room.

"Is there something wrong?" Nelle asked as she walked over to him.

Dutch didn't know what to say. So he just shook his head and said, "No."

"Then go back to bed," Nelle said as she turned back the covers and helped Dutch into bed. She tucked the covers in around him and kissed him good night.

And then all was quiet. There was no more shouting.

The next evening Jack was not at home when Nelle made the big pan of popcorn and put it on the table. She got out their book to read, but instead she laid it down on the table. She hesitated for only a moment, and then she said slowly, as if it were difficult for her to say, "Your father sometimes drinks whiskey, even though it is not good for him. But you should not hold this against him. We need to love and help him. Drinking too much alcohol can be a sickness, which some people cannot help."

Dutch didn't know exactly what his mother was talking about. The next day he looked carefully at his tall, handsome father and he didn't think he looked sick. He thought about how people liked to go into Pitney's General Store to buy shoes and other things because everyone liked Jack. Whenever there was a group of men standing around talking, they would always have a good time listening to Jack tell his funny stories.

One morning Nelle called to Dutch to come quickly. Dutch ran down the stairs wondering what was wrong. He ran into the kitchen saying, "What's wrong?"

"Nothing's wrong! Come and see what we have! Guinevere had kittens!"

Dutch ran over to see three little kittens in a box by the stove, and Guinevere curled around them. They were so cute, just little round balls of fur mewing and cuddling up to

Guinevere. Dutch named them King Arthur, Sir Galahad, and Buster.

Mr. Pitney finally sold his store in Tampico and gave Jack Reagan part ownership in another business he owned, the Fashion Boot Shop in Dixon. Jack told the boys over and over about the big city where they were moving. He told them about the fine house where they would be living and the large yard and barn. And he told them how the circus came to Dixon. They were so excited they could hardly wait.

On December 6, 1920, the Reagan family set off for Dixon, twenty-six miles to the north and east of Tampico. They all piled into their very first car, which had previously belonged to Mr. Pitney. Dutch brought Guinevere out to the car and he started to go back to get the kittens when Jack said, "Put Guinevere down, she is staying here."

Dutch couldn't believe what his father

was saying and he persisted, "We have to take Guinevere and her kittens! We can't leave them here! What would happen to them?"

"I am sorry," Jack replied, "but we just don't have room for four cats. They'll be fine here."

"How could they be fine!" Dutch frowned. "They're *our* cats, we have to take them." He looked pleadingly at his mother for her help, but she didn't say anything.

Jack said, "Go ahead and get in, Dutch."

Still protesting, he climbed into the back-seat of the car. Then he saw Nelle. She said nothing, but quietly she put the cat and her kittens in a basket and covered them with a linen towel. After the boys climbed into the car, she put the basket on the floor of the car and they put their feet on top of it.

The trip seemed long and they were so impatient. Neil and Dutch kept asking, "How soon will we be there?" Finally they drove down the street into Dixon and under a great arch with the letters D I X O N spelled across it!

Chapter Six

The Reagans moved into the nice big house at 816 Hennepin Avenue and Jack Reagan went to work at the Fashion Boot Shop, which he owned with Mr. Pitney. Dutch and Neil went to school at the South Side School, where Dutch was in the fifth grade and Neil in the seventh grade. Neil's friends at school nicknamed him "Moon," because they thought he looked like a cartoon character, *Moon Mullins*. This was fine with Neil, and after that everyone called him Moon.

The new house had a fine parlor with a

fireplace and a back sitting room where they sat to read or talk. The dining room had windows on the south side of the house, where the sunshine would pour in. The kitchen was large and had running water and an icebox. Up the steep staircase there were three bedrooms and a bathroom. Nelle and Jack had the largest bedroom. Dutch and Neil shared a small bedroom and the third bedroom was Nelle's sewing room, which was also used for guests sometimes.

Because the Reagan family had moved so often they didn't have much furniture. There were two things Nelle had always wanted, a sewing machine and a cabinet for her dishes, which had been a wedding present. Finally in Dixon she got her sewing machine *and* the china cabinet.

Dutch always loved to play outdoors. On hot summer days Dutch and some of his new friends would run to play in the forest along the magnificent Rock River. The trees were tall and massive, and the paths along the river covered with a thick blanket of leaves. The boys would climb back into the underbrush and imagine how it was when the Indians lived here. They watched the birds flying among the trees, like brief glimpses of color as they darted among the branches and then soared between the trees up into the blue sky. The boys would crouch under the underbrush of the forest, and pretend they were hiding from unknown enemies. They could hear small noises of animals scurrying on the forest floor, and sometimes a slim little snake would slide across their path to hide in the safety of the ground cover.

Everything in the cool, green forest was exciting. Dutch had read everything he could about the birds and wildlife of the Rock River valley. He had read about the early explorers from France and England who had explored from the Great Lakes through Illinois and down the Mississippi, trading with the Indians as they went. He also had read about the Indians and the Black Hawk War here in Illinois.

The boys pretended they were Indians as they silently roamed in the forest. They gathered at a small clearing near the river. The sounds of the forest were muted and they could hear the music of the waters of the Rock River flowing along its banks.

Dutch said, "You know that right here in Dixon, Black Hawk, one of the Sauk leaders, met with John Dixon."

One of the boys said, "Was the town Dixon here then?"

"No, only John Dixon was here, and he ran a ferry to cross the Rock River. He also had a store, bank, inn, and a post office in this log house," Dutch replied. "He founded the town of Dixon."

"What were Black Hawk and the Indians doing here?"

"Black Hawk told John Dixon that they

wanted to settle down and farm on Potawatomi land, which was a little east," Dutch answered. "But it didn't work out that way."

"What happened?"

"It turned out to be the Black Hawk War. Black Hawk and his band of Indians traveled all along the Rock River to Wisconsin and finally to Bad Axe, where there was a battle."

"Didn't Abe Lincoln fight in that battle?"

Dutch shook his head. "No, he was stationed with his volunteer company here in Dixon, but he wasn't ever in any fighting."

One of the boys asked, "How do you know all this?"

"We studied it in school . . . and I read about it," Dutch answered.

At first, Dutch spent a lot of his time reading or by himself. The boys in Dixon were friendly and he found lots of playmates, but it was slow for Dutch to make really close friends.

One of the first things Dutch did, when they moved to Dixon, was to sign up for a number at the library, which is the way the Dixon Library lent books. He borrowed at least two books every week. He would stretch out on the floor in the living room, and with his face just inches away from the book, read for hours at a time. He liked adventure stories. He read the Tarzan books and was carried off in his imagination to the jungle with Tarzan swinging from tree to tree. He especially liked the Frank Merriwell series, so well that he often read the books over again.

Nelle gave him a book, *Northern Lights*, about the white wolves of the north. Dutch read it again and again, and he imagined how it would be to live with the wolves in the wild. She also had a book with Robert Service's poem, "The Shooting of Dan McGrew." Dutch read it so many times that he had it memorized.

Though the parlor was usually closed off

with doors and saved for only very special occasions, one hot day Dutch stretched out on the floor to read. He lay by the ceramic tile hearth, and as he read, he ran his hand back and forth along the cool tiles. Suddenly he came to a rough spot where there was an uneven tile. He sat up and leaned over close to the tile so that he could see. The tile was loose, and with a little pressure on one side of the small tile, he flipped it up. At first he felt bad that he had somehow spoiled the ceramic hearth, and then he thought how clever it would be to have a secret tile where something could be hidden. He ran to tell Nelle about his discovery, and that night before they sat down to their evening popcorn and reading, the whole family gathered at the fireplace in the parlor.

Dutch lifted up the tile and Nelle said, "We can each put a penny under the tile." She handed a shiny copper penny to each of the boys and Jack and kept one for herself.

With great ceremony, Dutch put his penny down, then Neil, and Jack put his penny down with a flourish. Nelle put the fourth penny down and then carefully placed the tile over the four pennies. "Now we will never be penniless!" she declared dramatically. Dutch looked at the tile with satisfaction. It looked just like all the other tiles. It was a secret no one else would ever guess.

Sometimes Dutch and Neil called their parents by their first names and sometimes Mother and Dad. One evening as they were all sitting around the table in the sitting room, Neil suggested that they call their parents Nelle and Jack all the time, instead of Mother and Dad. They all agreed, and after that Dutch and Neil always called their parents Nelle and Jack.

On Sundays, Nelle and Dutch went to the Christian church, which met in the basement of the YMCA that first year they lived in

Dixon. Then later the church moved to a new building at Second and Hennepin, just a few blocks from their house. Though Jack and Neil usually went to the Catholic Church, many times Neil went with his mother and Dutch to church. Dutch and Neil were both baptized at the Christian church just a few days after the new church was opened.

Nelle was very busy in her church work. As she always had, Nelle spent her free hours helping other people. She visited patients at the mental hospital regularly, and each week Nelle took her Bible and went down to read to the prisoners in the county jail. Many people and especially youngsters didn't like to walk past the jail, because oftentimes the prisoners would stand at the windows and shout at passersby through the bars. Nelle did not hesitate to go in to sit with the prisoners and read to them from her Bible. For the most part the prisoners were young men who had been in fights or perhaps were thieves, but none of them were hardened criminals.

Sometimes when a prisoner was released from jail, he would not have anyplace to go. Several times Nelle would take a young man home and let him sleep in her sewing room for the night until he could find a place to stay.

Their evenings were as they always had been. They all sat around the table and Nelle read aloud to Dutch and Neil as they ate their delicious popcorn.

Then there was one evening that was quite different. The early evening was very dark and cold with a heavy snow on the ground. When eleven-year-old Dutch came running up the front steps, the house was dark. His mother was not yet home, and Neil was not there yet either.

Dutch ran up the snow-covered steps and onto the porch, which was blanketed with drifting snow. As he ran toward the door he stumbled over something lying in front of the door.

Dutch was shocked! When he leaned over to see what it was, he could see that it was his own father lying in the snow! His heart pounded at the fright. His father's eyes were closed, but he knew he was alive because he could hear him breathing heavily. He thought Jack must be terribly ill. He knelt down beside his father to see what he could do, and then he smelled the strong odor of whiskey! He didn't know what to do! He felt so mixed up . . . he felt sorry for his father, who looked so pitiful lying in the snow, and yet he felt a kind of anger. How could Jack do this!

He tried to wake Jack, but his father's head rolled to the side, his mouth fell open, and he snored so loudly that Dutch was sure the neighbors would hear. He didn't know what to do. His first thought was to step over Jack and go on in the house and up to his own room.

Then he knew there was no one else to help, and he couldn't leave his father in the cold snow. He stepped over Jack's body and opened the front door. He grabbed Jack's coat collar and dragging him by his coat, managed to pull him into the house.

Chapter Seven

The next morning Neil and Dutch were at the breakfast table when Jack came bounding down the stairs. Dutch felt a little uncomfortable when he saw his father. He dropped his eyes and wondered what his father would say, but it was just as if nothing had ever happened. After a good night's rest in bed, Jack was his own handsome, hearty self again. He didn't appear to remember any of what had happened the night before. Jack had his breakfast as he always did and after kissing Nelle, and patting each of the boys on their heads, strode out the front door on his way to work.

That night Nelle again talked to the boys about how they must love and respect their father, who was a very fine man. It was only that he was not able to drink liquor, which was a kind of illness. As winter waned and spring arrived, and his father was his own normal self, Dutch almost forgot that snowy night. At least it seemed somehow far away, and he didn't want to think about it.

Living in Dixon was exciting. Sometimes on a Friday night the whole family would go to the movies. Dutch was really happy when the movie was a western. He loved to watch Tom Mix, William S. Hart, and all the other cowboy stars in their films where they were so brave and courageous and always saved the beautiful girls after they won the fights with the bad guys. Dutch would lose himself in his imagination, as he could just feel the pleasure of riding horseback as the cowboy hero galloped along the dusty trails on his trusted horse.

Then on Saturday nights everyone went down to town. Nelle and Dutch and Moon always went downtown, but Jack didn't go with them because he needed to work in the Fashion Boot Shop, which was open on Saturday nights. He hoped that there would be a lot of people who would need new shoes. He was very skilled in fitting shoes properly, no matter what problems people had with their feet. He had taken several correspondence courses to learn about fitting shoes. The Fashion Boot Shop had the most up-to-date equipment, including an X-ray machine. The customer could try on a new shoe, place his foot in the X-ray machine, and then look down through the viewing device to see his foot bones in the shoe! Jack wondered whether some of the customers really wanted to buy shoes, or whether they just wanted to try the novelty of the X-ray machine.

The farmers would come in from the surrounding area to shop and see their friends. Many of the townspeople would drive their cars down in the late afternoon, find a good parking place, and then go home to eat their supper. When they walked back in the evening, they could sit in their cars and have a parking place where they could see and be seen. It was just like a big get-together. Nelle, Dutch, and Moon would walk down to town. Nelle would stop to talk to her friends and Dutch and Moon would run along, darting in and out among the people standing on the sidewalk. Moon ran on down Galena Street to catch up with the O'Malley boys, but Dutch lingered around the courthouse, where the old men gathered to talk about the wars and the times that Abraham Lincoln came to Dixon.

There was one old soldier, who was almost always there in the group. He loved to talk about the Civil War days and President

Abraham Lincoln. He was very distinguished with snow-white hair and a white flowing mustache. He was very tall and straight and always wore a military cap and an ancient blue military jacket. He was ready to talk with anyone who wanted to listen. He usually was at the center of the Civil War veterans as they stood exchanging stories with one another.

The old man's eyes narrowed as he watched Dutch read the plaque on the courthouse lawn, which said: LINCOLN STOOD HERE WHILE DELIVERING HIS GREAT SPEECH, JULY 17, 1856.

"You know, I heard Abraham Lincoln deliver that speech right here on this lawn. He spoke for nearly two hours. I was a boy, not much older than you."

Dutch marveled at that, he couldn't imagine the old man ever being a boy. And he had trouble imagining that President Abraham Lincoln had ever been right here on this very spot. "That was before Lincoln was president, wasn't it?"

"Yes, he was giving a speech for the election of John C. Freemont for president. That was in 1856 and, as you know, Lincoln wasn't elected president until later in 1860.

"Abe Lincoln was here in Dixon several times," the old veteran went on. "You know that he stayed over at the Nachusa House." Dutch looked over at the old hotel, the Nachusa House.

Dutch started to walk on, when the old man said, "Did I ever tell you that I served under General Ulysses S. Grant?" Dutch stopped to listen. "I was at the Battle of Shiloh in April of 1862 . . . one of the bloodiest battles of the war!"

The old veteran shook his head and frowned as he said, "That's where I got this gimpy leg. I was in the finest outfit there was . . . but we sure left a lot of boys there on that battlefield."

Another of the old soldiers added, "I signed up for the Illinois Volunteers with Ulysses Grant, when he was just a captain in Galena, Illinois."

"Yep, and before that he worked as a clerk in his father's leather goods shop there in Galena. But he sure was one fine general and commander of the Union army. And of course you know that Ulysses S. Grant was the eighteenth president of the United States." His blue eyes were piercing under his bushy white eyebrows as he looked straight at Dutch.

Dutch nodded as he thought how important Illinois was to have two men who had become president of the United States. He liked to talk with these old men who knew so much of the past. It was like listening to real history.

He hated to leave, but he decided he had better catch up with Moon and his mother. Nelle was on down the street a ways talking with some of her friends from church.

On summer nights oftentimes Nelle would take the boys down by the river to stop in Fulf's, the sweet shop where they sold home-made ice cream. Dutch didn't want to be left out, in case that was where Nelle was going.

When he reached Nelle, she said, "You are just in time. I thought we would go for ice cream, if you want to."

Dutch grinned from ear to ear. As if there was any doubt! Fulf's was crowded as it always was on a summer Saturday night. Finally it was their turn and the fountain man scooped up the dips of ice cream and placed them firmly on the cones. He handed one to Neil, one to Dutch, and one to Nelle.

They walked on down the street with their cones in hand. Dutch ate his delicious ice cream cone as slowly as he could to make it last. There was a feeling of excitement in the air, as they strolled along in the long evening twilight. Then finally as darkness fell, the streetlights came on and after a while the people started to go home, and one after another the parked cars would leave. Then Nelle and the boys would walk home slowly. Being in town on Saturday night was so special, they were sorry for it to come to an end.

In the fall after the days became a little cooler, Dutch and Moon played football with their friends, the O'Malley boys, who lived across the street. Eddie and Dutch were the same age and George O'Malley and Moon were in the same class at school. Usually Eddie and Dutch played George and Moon. Wink McReynolds, Moon's best friend, often played with them and other friends would join the rough and tumble games. They played on the Reagans' side lawn. Many times as they were playing in the Reagans' yard, the ball would be thrown or kicked into the garden of the ladies who lived next door.

Since Dutch was always friendly and courteous, the two older ladies particularly liked him, so the other boys always sent Dutch to get the ball. He would try to walk through the garden carefully, but it wasn't easy to go through the garden without stepping on some of the flowers.

As Dutch went after the football, one of the ladies came out on the porch. She drew herself up very tall and slim. She took a deep breath as she said, "Dutch, please don't let your friends throw the ball into our flowers." And she glared at the other boys who were waiting for Dutch to retrieve their ball.

Dutch mumbled, "I'm sorry," as he climbed back over the fence. With their constant running and sliding as they played, their yard became either a dust bowl or a mud hole depending on the sun or rain. Finally one day Jack came out, shook his head at the boys, and said, "Why don't you go over to the O'Malleys and ruin their yard for a while."

The neighbor ladies nodded their heads at each other. They were so pleased that Jack

Reagan had told the boys to move the football playing field across the street. They thought the move away from their garden was not a moment too soon!

When wintertime came, the boys could hardly wait until it was cold enough for the Rock River to freeze, and when it did, they had the grandest ice to skate upon. Dutch and Moon and their friends glided up the river as fast as they could skate. Then they would hold their coats out like sails so that the wind would blow them back down river. Then sometimes they would play a fast, rollicking game of hockey!

In the summer they fished in the river, went swimming, and played in the woods of Lowell Park. Sometimes they pretended they were the early explorers floating down the Rock River, as they went out in canoes.

One Sunday, Jack took the family for an afternoon drive through the countryside around Dixon. Dutch and Moon sat in the backseat and Nelle was in front with Jack. As they drove along, Moon read all the signs aloud. Many of the barns had advertising signs on them and he also read any billboard signs he saw. Dutch didn't know how Moon could read the words as they drove past. The signs were all just blurs to Dutch!

Dutch picked up Nelle's glasses, which she had left on the backseat. Just for fun he put them on. As he looked out of the car, the letters on the signboard came into clear view. He gave a shriek!

"What's wrong!" Jack shouted as he slammed on the brakes.

Dutch saw things he had never seen before! He could see leaves on the trees, which before were just hazy green shapes. He could even read the words on the billboards!

He had just discovered how nearsighted he was!

The next day Nelle took him to get big,

black-rimmed glasses with thick glass lenses. Nelle was shocked to learn how badly he needed them. No wonder he had always put his nose in a book in order to read, and that he always wanted to sit in the front row at school! Dutch was so glad to be able to see with his new glasses, but after a while he hated the way the glasses looked on him.

Dutch loved sports and now with his new glasses, he could see well enough to even hit a baseball! He liked other activities as well. When a boys band was started in Dixon, Dutch wanted to be in that too, though he didn't play an instrument. He practiced and practiced baton twirling with an old broomstick, and ended up being the drum major, who would lead the band!

The band marched in the Decoration Day parade in Amboy, a nearby small town. The Dixon Boys Band was to be the first in the parade right behind the parade marshal on his horse. The boys looked very sharp in their band uniforms, and Dutch led the band proudly pumping his baton up and down to the rhythm of the drums. They marched down the middle of the street, and at one point the marshall turned around and rode back down the parade line to make sure everyone was coming along. Leading the parade, Dutch kept marching down the street, but after a while he noticed that the music was getting fainter and fainter. When he turned around, there was no band following! The marshall had returned to lead the parade down a cross street and the band had followed him! Dutch was marching all alone!

When he realized he was going the wrong way he ran back. The crowds along the way laughed and clapped for him, as he caught up to take his place at the head of the band again.

Chapter Eight

Each summer the Chautauqua would come to Dixon. The Chatauqua was a series of programs, which lasted all day long with speakers and performers over a two-week period. The name, Chatauqua, came from a town in upstate New York where these gatherings were first held.

It was such an exciting time for Dixon. The speakers came from all over the country and everyone for miles around would come into town to see and hear all the marvelous programs. Nelle looked forward each year to going to the Chatauqua and to taking Dutch with her. When Nelle had read in the newspaper, the *Dixon Telegraph*, that the Chatauqua was coming, she told Dutch that they would go one of the days when it was held in Dixon. Dutch was really glad to go to the Chatauqua with Nelle.

The day finally came and Nelle and Dutch took the trolley to the end of the line to the Assembly grounds where the program was to be held. They sat at a picnic table in the clear, bright sunshine to eat their lunch of apples and crackers, which Nelle had brought with her. They looked at all the people milling about, waiting for the show to start.

Nelle and Dutch drank in the atmosphere of excitement. They talked to some of the other people who had come to hear the program and listened to all the comments about who was going to speak, and what the subjects were. Gradually people started to go into the big Assembly Hall.

It was wonderful to have all these speakers come to Dixon. Some of them were staying at the Nachusa House in Dixon, but most of them stayed here at the lodge on the Assembly grounds. Dutch looked around. He wondered if he could see any of the people who would be on the program. He asked Nelle, "Do you think any of the speakers are out here?"

She shook her head. "No, I'm sure they are backstage getting ready for their presentations. You know how that is. When you are going before an audience, you need to concentrate on your preparation."

After they finished their lunch they went into the large Assembly Hall and took their seats. They listened intently to the speakers who talked about religion and the importance of living a godly life. Some of the speakers were preachers who really gave sermons. And then there were speakers who read from the Bible in many different ways.

Some of the speakers were very dramatic, presenting the Bible readings almost as if they were acting out a play in a theater. Nelle was very impressed with the talents of the performers, and she got some ideas for her own presentations to her church groups.

Then the next program was simply amazing and wondrous! Dutch was entranced with the presentation of an entertainer named Louis Williams who gave demonstrations of electricity. He showed how messages could be sent through wireless telegraphy, as he would tap out the Morse code from one telegrapher to be received at the other end by another telegrapher. He had experiments, which were very compelling, with wires that lit up, and some of the demonstrations were almost frightening, such as when the vacuum tube that Williams held in his hand lit with random streaks of light glimmering from one of the tubes to the other!

Dutch was so intent on listening and

watching all these strange and marvelous demonstrations! The programs of the Chatauqua were so very special to Dutch. It was like a whole different world from his ordinary, daily life.

Dutch spent a lot of time with his friends from church. Many times a group of friends would go to Howard Hall's house to listen to the radio. Although Dutch was quite a bit younger than the rest of this group, he liked to go along because he was so interested in Howard's radio. Howard would turn on his crystal radio set, which he had built himself. The radio stations were not on all day, and so they would all sit and wait for the chimes of WOC, which signaled that the radio station was on the air.

It was such a thrill when, after waiting silently for such a long time, they finally heard the chimes! Dutch exclaimed, "Oh, listen, WOC is on the air!"

Gladys, one of the older girls, said, "Shsh . . . Dutch, we can't hear!" They had to sit so quietly so they could hear the announcer saying, "This is WOC Davenport!"

Dutch and Neil were good friends, but their activities were very different. Dutch went with his mother to church and to the church activities and spent much of his time with his Sunday school friends. His Sunday school class got paid for doing the janitor's work at church, and they used the money to plaster their Sunday school classroom.

Neil hung with a different group of friends, who, after school, sometimes played pool in a basement pool hall, where they couldn't be seen from the street. Dutch wasn't invited to go with his brother's friends and their activities.

Even though Nelle was very careful in the way she spent money, there never seemed to be enough money to meet all their bills. She always did her part in trying to stretch their money. The family usually had their dinner, the largest meal of the day at noon, and often that was oatmeal hamburger. She would cook a panful of oatmeal and mix it with cooked hamburger and make it into patties. She served the round patties in gravy, which she made from cooking the hamburger. It was delicious and the boys loved it.

But, by the end of the summer, Jack decided that the rent on their house on Hennepin Avenue was too expensive, so they moved to a smaller house at 338 West Everett on the north side of town. Dutch and Moon slept on a porch, which had windows but no heat. This was very comfortable in the summer, but it was more than a little chilly in the winter. Their new house overlooked the football field, and Dutch would watch the high-school boys practicing and dream about when he would be big enough to play high-school football.

Since they now lived on the north side of town, Dutch went to North Dixon High School. Moon continued to go to South Dixon High School, since he had gone there for two years and was a junior. The two schools had only one combined football team. Moon was a big, strong boy and a natural athlete, and he and his best friend, Wink McReynolds played on the football team.

Dutch tried out for football, although at thirteen he was not very tall and he was scrawny. He wanted so much to play, but he sat on the bench for his first two years on the team. In the summer of 1925, Dutch had a growing spurt and he also gained weight. He turned into a tall, muscular young man and finally made the second string in his third year in high school.

That summer, when the Ringling Brothers Circus came rolling into town, one of their friends ran past, saying, "I heard that the circus is hiring kids to help with setting up."

Quickly Moon and Dutch ran down to where the circus was unloading and they got jobs. They were to be paid twenty-five cents an hour as roustabouts, which meant they would do whatever they were asked to do in getting the circus set up. As the circus settled into Demon Town, their first job was to pull the heavy circus wagons into place in the mud, so they would not roll.

Then the next day they had to be on the job at four o'clock in the morning to feed the elephants because it was the elephants who pulled the ropes to raise the tents. It was a sight to behold, and both boys were amazed as they saw how everyone worked together to get the circus set up. In addition to their pay, they were given tickets so they and their friends could come to see the circus and the spectacular acts under the big top.

After the circus left town, Dutch got a job with a building contractor doing hard physical labor. He was glad to get the job, not only for the money, but to make himself strong and tougher for football. He got thirty-five cents an hour for working ten hours a day, six days a week. The job was digging the foundation for the new Catholic church.

One day Jack came by at noon to take him home for dinner. Dutch had just raised his pickax when the noon whistle blew. When he saw his father, he did not put the pickax down carefully. He just dropped it! The heavy pickax almost hit the foot of the boss, who was very angry and shouted at Jack, "Your kid can get less dirt on a shovel than anyone I know!" But he didn't fire Dutch. And, in fact, Dutch earned nearly two hundred dollars that summer, which he saved for college.

Though Dutch was working very hard all week, he still went to church every Sunday with his mother, where he taught a Sunday school class of boys only two or three years younger than he was. Lamar Wells, Ken Detweiler, and the other boys never missed either, because they loved to hear Dutch read from the Bible.

Chapter Nine

The next year Dutch got the best job of his young life, when he applied for the job of lifeguard at the Rock River beach in Lowell Park. Jack was reading the paper when Dutch came down for breakfast. "There was another drowning at Lowell Park yesterday."

Nelle hesitated in putting the oatmeal on the table as she exclaimed, "Oh, dear, who was it?"

Jack read on, "It was a young man from Ohio, who was visiting friends here in Dixon."

Nelle shook her head in sympathy. "How sad . . . I certainly feel for his family."

"There have been so many drownings at Lowell Park that the Park District is considering closing the swimming area."

Dutch sat down at the breakfast table. He helped himself to a bowl of oatmeal as he said, "They shouldn't close the beach. They need to get a good lifeguard."

Jack looked up from his newspaper and said, "Dutch, you're a good swimmer, maybe that would be a good job for you. Let's go up to the park and see if they will hire you as a lifeguard."

And so Jack drove Dutch up to the park where Dutch applied for the job to Mr. and Mrs. Graybill, who ran the concession at the swimming area.

Ruth Graybill looked at Dutch and said, "I think you are right. We *do* need a lifeguard if we are going to keep the swimming beach open." She shook her head. "But aren't you too young to be a lifeguard?"

"Give him a chance," Jack Reagan said in his most persuasive salesman's voice. "He can do it!"

So, in the end, Mrs. Graybill gave him the job for the summer. "Your pay will be fifteen dollars a week, and all the nickel root beers and ten-cent hamburgers from the concession stand that you can eat."

That sounded good to Dutch.

"You will be on duty from ten in the morning to ten at night . . . every day . . . seven days a week."

But his day started much earlier. In the morning he walked over to the Graybills' house, which was just across the street from South Central School. He helped Mrs. Graybill pack up the food supplies for the day and they picked up ice for the coolers. Then they would drive out to the park in the Graybills' old Ford truck. When they got there, he would help her unload the food and

put the ice in the icebox and in the drink coolers. When he finished unloading, he would get into his swimsuit and climb up on the lifeguard stand. The job was perfect for Dutch. He loved it and everyone liked him!

Dutch watched the river carefully as all the kids splashed and swam about. In the morning, if he had time, he would help the younger children learn how to swim. The Rock River was a treacherous place to swim. The bottom sloped down abruptly and the water became quite deep. Also sometimes, because of a dam downstream, the current suddenly became stronger and faster. The river was nearly six hundred feet wide at that point, and if a swimmer started across, he or she had to go the whole way, because there was no place to stop midstream. Dutch taught himself to watch for any unusual activity, but especially two or three places where trouble occurred most often.

When he had time to leave his lifeguard

stand, which wasn't often, Dutch swam. He would dive off the board with a beautiful dive and glide through the water with strong, graceful strokes. He loved the cool fresh water as he swam along swiftly and smoothly.

That very first summer, Dutch pulled several swimmers out of the river when they were in danger of drowning. His father told him that he should make notches in a log so that he could keep a tally of how many people he had saved. So he did. He pulled up a big, old log and made a notch in the log, for each time he pulled a struggling swimmer from the river.

After a while the swimmers at the beach would check his log to see how many notches there were. Each summer there were more and more notches added on the log. And there was never a drowning during any of the summers that Dutch was a lifeguard!

That winter in high school was a great time

for Dutch. He got to play football, because he was now five feet ten and a half inches tall and weighed more than 160 pounds. He was finally big enough to play football! Though he was now on the varsity team, he was still on the bench. At last, one Saturday morning, as the coach was reading the starting lineup, he called, "Right guard, Reagan!"

Dutch wanted to leap up from his bench and shout! From that game on, Dutch had the first-string job for the rest of the season.

That year there were two new important changes in town. The Christian church had a new minister, Reverend Ben Cleaver. And there was also a new English teacher, B. J. Frazer, at the high school. Each of these men had a strong influence on Dutch in his growing years.

Dutch went to church every Sunday with Nelle except for those Sundays in the summer when he had to be on his lifeguard stand at the Rock River beach in Lowell Park. He listened to Reverend Cleaver's sermons, though sometimes it was difficult not to become distracted. It did not take Dutch very long to notice Reverend Cleaver's three pretty daughters, and in particular, Margaret. She was very pretty with auburn hair and was also very smart. In church, Dutch kept looking over his hymnal at Margaret.

As Margaret and Dutch became friends, Dutch found all kinds of excuses to go to the Cleavers' house. So Dutch not only saw and heard Reverend Cleaver at church, he also saw a good deal of him at his home. Reverend Ben Cleaver liked Dutch and enjoyed talking to him.

The new English teacher, B. J. Frazer, wore glasses almost as thick as Dutch's. It was from Mr. Frazer that Dutch first learned about acting. And he discovered that he loved acting as much as he loved swimming and football.

Mr. Frazer changed the way they studied

English. In the past their essays in English class had been graded only for spelling and grammar. Mr. Frazer announced that he was going to grade also on the originality of their writing. This led Dutch to use his imagination and creativity in his writings. Soon Mr. Frazer had Dutch read some of his essays to the class. When the class enjoyed what he had written and would laugh at his jokes, he started writing to entertain his classmates. He found he enjoyed it as much as the readings he had done with his mother at her programs.

Mr. Frazer staged complete plays at the high school. Dutch learned acting techniques from Mr. Frazer, which he always remembered. Mr. Frazer never told the students how to read their lines, but rather that it was important to learn about the characters they were playing and to try to think like them. Then when the actor was on the stage, he could really *be* that person.

Dutch and Margaret were both in many of the dramatic productions. In their junior year they were in the junior class play, *You and I*. And as seniors Dutch and Margaret were in the senior class play, *Captain Applejack*.

Sometimes when Dutch was studying his lines for a play, he would go into his own chilly sleeping porch bedroom and stretch out on the bed. It was easy for him to memorize. He would look at the page for only a few moments and he could remember the whole page. And then his thoughts would wander and he would think about how lucky he was. He loved playing football, and he loved being in the school plays with Mr. Frazer as his drama coach. It was great being at North Dixon High School. In addition to playing football, he was on the track team. He was in the Drama Club, and was president of the club in his senior year. He was on the Annual staff and vice president of the hi Y. And then he thought about how he had been elected president of the North High School student body. He felt good about school, his friends, and all his activities, football, drama, and just everything!

After Dutch graduated from high school in the summer of 1928, he again worked as a lifeguard. One evening after the beach was closed, Ed Graybill and Dutch were closing the bathhouse for the night. Suddenly they heard screaming and thrashing about in the water. Dutch whirled about and saw a swimmer splashing and going under into very deep water. Another swimmer was trying to rescue him, and he was being taken under by the drowning man. Dutch immediately dived into the water and swiftly swam to the two men, who were sinking under the water. As Dutch grabbed the drowning man, the second man was able to free himself and swim to safety. After a struggle, Dutch was able to subdue the drowning man and pull him to shore. Quickly, once on shore, Dutch gave him artificial respiration. He soon came around, and after a short time recovered enough so that his friends could take him to his home.

The *Dixon Telegraph* the next day carried an article with the headline DROWNING VICTIM PULLED FROM JAWS OF DEATH and the article reported that "lifeguard Ronald Reagan rescued a man from drowning last night about nine thirty, making his twenty-fifth rescue at the beach in the past two seasons."

Chapter Ten

Dutch climbed up on the lifeguard's stand, after the concession stand was stocked with all the food supplies and the ice. Though the August sun was already hot at 10:00 A.M., he liked being up there. He almost felt like he was on stage.

Dutch was very tanned with sunbleached hair. Although he was intent on watching all the swimmers to make sure they were safe, he looked comfortably at ease as he sat on the edge of the lifeguard's chair with his long brown legs dangling to the footrest. Many of the girls thought he was so handsome that he almost looked like a movie star.

Some of the girls, who wanted to be friendly, would gather around the lifeguards' stand to talk to Dutch, but he only had eyes for Margaret Cleaver. Some evenings after the beach was closed, they would go out on the river in a canoe.

One sultry summer evening Dutch and Margaret planned to go boating on the Rock River, and the swimmers stayed and stayed. Dutch had given them fair warning, as he had called out that it was ten o'clock and the beach was closed for the night.

The night was hot and the water was cool, so the swimmers were in no hurry to get out of the water. They laughed and played as they continued to splash and swim in the cool water.

Margaret looked at Dutch and smiled as she said, "I think we might as well forget about going out boating tonight. I don't think those kids are going to come out of the water."

Dutch grinned. "You just watch." With that he picked up a pebble and threw it skipping across the water. Then he called out, "Don't worry, that is just a rat swimming by." That got the swimmers out of the water in a hurry!

After the swimmers had left, Dutch pushed the canoe out. He helped Margaret in, shoved the canoe into the water, and jumped in. The moon cast a romantic ribbon of light on the dark water of the Rock River. Dutch dipped the oars easily, and they enjoyed floating in their canoe through the silvery waters of the river.

They talked about their plans. Margaret was going to Eureka College when school started in the fall. Dutch wanted to go to college also, but he wasn't sure about the money he would need.

"Daddy is going to be driving me down to college, and you could go too," Margaret said.

Dutch was serious as he said, "I figure that I'll have four hundred dollars saved by the end of summer. Do you think that will be enough?"

Margaret was reassuring. "Go down and talk to the dean. Maybe you can get a scholarship or a job or something. My sister said that her boyfriend is a Teke (fraternity member), and you can probably stay at their frat house."

In 1928 not many graduating high-school seniors went on to college, but Dutch never doubted that he would. Both Reverend Cleaver and B. J. Frazer had encouraged Dutch to continue his education. And Nelle Reagan felt it was very important that both of her sons go on to college, although Neil had not thought college was important and had gotten a job after high school.

Dutch had never seen Eureka College, but he knew that was where he wanted to go. One of the football stars from Dixon High

School, Garland Waggoner, whom Dutch had admired, had gone on to play football at Eureka. Margaret's two older sisters went there and, of course, Margaret was going to Eureka.

In September, Reverend Cleaver drove Margaret to Eureka to enroll in school and Dutch rode along. As they drove up to the college campus, Dutch couldn't believe his eyes. He took a deep breath as he looked at the large ivy-covered red brick buildings, which were set in a semicircle among huge, majestic trees on a rolling green lawn. He fell in love with Eureka. It looked just like a college ought to look!

He felt his heart quicken. He wanted to go to this college so badly. He just hoped he had enough money. Slowly he walked into the dean's office, and a pleasant young lady asked him to wait. While he waited the palms of his hands grew moist, as he thought about what he wanted to say to the dean.

Though it seemed he had waited a long time, after about ten minutes Dean Harrod came to the door of his office and invited Dutch in. After a very short conversation, Dean Harrod offered him a scholarship for half of his tuition as well as a job washing dishes in a dormitory for his board. Dutch would only have to pay for his room and his books. He could have jumped for joy! It was an answer to a dream.

Dutch moved into the Teke house, as a pledge of the Tau Kappa Epsilon fraternity. He moved his belongings into the house and upstairs to the dorm room, where he sank down on the bed. He could scarcely believe his good fortune. He had a place to stay, a job to work for his meals, and tuition for school!

He could hardly wait to get started in school. Dutch went out for football, though he got no further than sitting on the bench, which was his one disappointment this first year at Eureka. Eureka College had only 250 students and it wasn't long until Dutch felt he knew almost everyone in school, either from his classes, Margaret and her friends, his job, or from his sports.

As it turned out Dutch was living in the most interesting place to be that fall. Because Eureka was a small school, and the country's economy was falling on hard times, the college was having trouble paying its bills. The president of the college decided the only way to keep the school from having to close because of a lack of money was to eliminate some of the classes and to reduce the number of faculty.

The Teke house was the center of a student strike asking for the resignation of the president of the Eureka College! Faculty and students alike wanted the president to resign because of his unpopular position on cutting back on classes in trying to save money. The upperclassmen were concerned that they would not be able to take the subjects they needed in order to graduate. Dutch and some 150 other students signed a petition asking that the president resign.

This petition asking for the president's resignation was taken to the board of trustees. The meeting lasted until midnight, and when the students learned that the trustees refused to ask for the president's resignation, the college bell began to toll.

The students, and many of the faculty, gathered at the chapel to protest. It was decided that a freshman should present the motion to call for a strike, and Dutch was the freshman chosen to do it.

It was the first time Dutch had ever made a speech before a large group like this. When he stood, at first he felt a little nervous, and then as he felt the approval of the crowd, he became more relaxed and confident. He talked on and on, describing what had happened. The president was going to cut out many of the classes and faculty members were going to lose their jobs. The board of trustees were backing the president, even though the students had asked for the resignation of the president. He announced that the plan of the group was not to go to classes until the president resigned. The response to his speech was so enthusiastic, that the crowd rose to their feet shouting their votes to strike. Dutch was exhilarated with being able to move an audience!

The students did not go to classes. The professors did go to their classes, and they marked all the students present, even though they were not in class. Finally the president did resign and the college classes continued. The students had won!

Dutch loved college life. He enjoyed walking through the campus with his best girl, Margaret, on warm evenings, with the smell of spring in the air, and ending up at the drugstore for a cherry phosphate (soda) or dancing with Margaret at the fraternity dances or talking with his friends at the Teke house until all hours. He enjoyed his classes and did moderately well. He was the star of the swimming team, but he was disappointed that it took two years before he finally made the football team. Those first two years, he was sure that Coach McKinzie didn't like him, but he learned from that experience.

After two years of working, Neil finally decided that he wanted to go to Eureka College too. Dutch talked to Coach McKinzie, who gave Neil an athletic scholarship. Dutch was delighted when Moon came to school with him, and it was interesting that the older brother was now behind his younger brother in school. And both brothers played football!

Dutch blocked and tackled as hard as he could during practice and continually tried to improve. One evening, as he was walking across campus, he saw Coach McKinzie who said, "Keep it up, Dutch! You're doing fine!"

Hearing those words made Dutch feel just great! And then one rainy day when they were practicing a new play, Coach McKinzie told Dutch to practice taking down the defensive halfback. One of the assistant coaches played the role of the defensive halfback. Dutch said, "You don't want me to really hit him?"

The assistant coach said, "Sure, do your best!"

Dutch threw a block like he had never done before, and he really hit the assistant coach like a ton of bricks! Coach McKinzie put his hand over his mouth to cover his smile, as the assistant coach limped off the field.

Coach McKinzie played Dutch in every game from then on!

✿ ✿ ✿

At Eureka College, Dutch found another wonderful drama coach, Miss Ellen Marie Johnson. Margaret and Dutch were both in the Dramatic Society and often had the leading roles in their plays. In their junior year Miss Johnson entered their drama group in the annual one-act play competition at Northwestern University's School of Speech. Out of the hundreds of colleges and universities that entered the competition, only twelve or so were selected to come to Northwestern to present their one-act plays. Eureka's drama group was very honored to be selected to participate.

The Eureka group rehearsed and rehearsed their play, *Aria da Capo*, in which Dutch and his friend Bud Cole played a pair of Greek shepherds. They were delighted when their play won second place, and Dutch was stunned to receive a prize for his individual performance!

Because of the depression, the Fashion

Boot Shop closed, and Jack had taken a job in a cheap shoe chain store in Springfield, Illinois. Nelle had gone to work in a dress shop for fourteen dollars a week in order to help out. All the family was home for the holidays that last Christmas vacation, when Dutch was a senior in college.

On Christmas Eve, as Dutch and Moon were planning to go out for the evening, a special delivery letter arrived for Jack. The family stood around as Jack opened the envelope and drew out a single sheet of blue paper. He didn't even raise his head as he said bleakly, "What a miserable Christmas present."

Jack was fired! He had lost his job!

Jack and Nelle could no longer afford the rent on their house so they moved to an apartment in the upstairs of a home. During his senior year, Dutch sent money home whenever he could.

❖   ❖   ❖

Dutch received a fine education in his four years at Eureka College, not only in academics, but also from his involvement in the college activities. He performed in seven plays, received varsity letters in both football and swimming, was president of the Booster club, and president of the student senate. He spent one year on the student newspaper, and two years on the yearbook staff and was elected senior class president.

The sun was bright and the sky blue on graduation day in June of 1932 at Eureka College, when Dutch gave his commencement speech as president of the senior class. He felt both happy and sad. He was joyful that he had graduated from college and he was aware of the pride his mother, Nelle, had in his achievement. But like the other students, he was uncertain about his next step in life. He knew from his own family about the lack of money with no job, or a job which paid so little. The country was going through

144

a very difficult time and he knew that jobs were not easy to find.

After graduation the forty-five graduates participated in a traditional ivy ceremony. They held long strands of ivy, which they cut to mark the parting of their ways. Margaret and Dutch held an uncut strand of ivy, signifying that their friendship would continue after college. Margaret got a job teaching and, despite the uncut strand, eventually their ways parted also.

Chapter Eleven

Dutch graduated from Eureka College at a time when the country was suffering from the Great Depression. Each month the situation grew worse. People did not have money to spend. For those people who were out of work, there were no jobs to be found. The Reagans had the same kind of problems that many people were having. Jack still had not been able to find a job, and Nelle was working at the job where she was paid very little. In order to make ends meet, they lived in only a small part of their apartment and rented out the rest of it. They cooked on a little hot plate in their bedroom. When Moon and Dutch came home, Moon slept on the couch and Dutch slept on a cot on the stair landing.

All over the country thousands of people did not have jobs and it was no different in Dixon. One by one the factories closed and the employees found themselves without jobs. Unemployed men and women wandered up and down the streets through town trying to find work in order to pay their rent and feed their families. Discouraged, oftentimes they just sat down on the benches, or even curbs, when they could go no farther. There was nowhere to go to get a job. A line of hungry, jobless people lined up each morning at Newman's Garage for free bread and hot coffee. Those people who were fortunate enough to still have a job or a little money would try to help their neighbors.

＊   ＊   ＊

Franklin Delano Roosevelt had been nominated by the Democratic Party for president
of the United States and was running against
President Herbert Hoover. Jack felt it was
very important to elect a new president, and
he was confident that Franklin Roosevelt
could get this country straightened out again.
And so Jack spent his time working for
Roosevelt's election.

Dutch came back home to Dixon after he
graduated from Eureka and spent the summer working as a lifeguard again. He was
glad to have the job! As he had all the summers before, he saved many lives. Dutch
watched the dark water carefully, and when
he saw someone in trouble in the water, in an
instant he flung his glasses on the ground,
and leaped from his lifeguard stand and into
the water.

One late afternoon a young man on the

diving tower slipped and fell, hitting his head against the ladder! Dutch saw him fall, and heard the screams of the swimmers who saw the accident. Dutch ran, plunged into the water, and swam quickly to the young man, who had sunk into the deep water. Dutch dived several times before he could reach the victim. Skillfully he placed his strong arm around the neck of the unconscious man, and dragged him to shore. People at the beach gathered around, watching and waiting, as Dutch revived the victim and got him breathing again.

There was a collective sigh of relief from the crowd, when it was clear that this was another life saved. One of the younger boys cried out, "Dutch, cut another notch in your lifesaving log!"

Dutch was catching his breath, as he was relieved that he had been able to save another life. He grabbed a towel and dried his face and then looked for his glasses. There were several kids standing around, and one of them ran to pick up his glasses and handed them to Dutch.

Another of the boys borrowed a pocket knife from a nearby man and said, "Dutch, can I cut the notch?"

Dutch nodded as he put on his glasses, and keeping his eyes on the crowd of swimmers in the river, climbed back on his stand.

The young boy carefully carved in a notch, and then he counted and announced proudly, "This is the seventy-first notch!"

One of the other kids marveled, "Dutch, is that right? Have you saved seventy-one lives?"

Dutch climbed back on the stand in his wet suit, as he heard the young boys talking. "However many notches are on the log . . . that's how many people I've pulled out of the river!"

"Do you ever go in just for fun to get some-one?"

Dutch laughed. "No, I'm not going to jump down off this stand and get my suit wet, if I don't have to!"

By the time the summer was over he had carved in the seventy-seventh notch. Over his seven seasons as a lifeguard at Lowell Park, Dutch Reagan had rescued seventy-seven people and there was not one drowning during that time!

As he had every year, he taught children to swim. He helped his friends who wanted to become better swimmers and divers. One high school friend, George Joyce, used to come out after work, and Dutch taught him to dive.

Dutch had many friends among the people who came to the park year after year. One man, Sid Altschuler, a successful businessman from Kansas City, brought his wife and two little girls back to Dixon each summer to visit their grandparents. And Dutch taught the girls how to swim.

Mr. Altschuler asked Dutch what he planned to do in the fall. Dutch answered, "I want to get a job, but the times are so bad."

"The depression is not going to last forever. Just take any job you can find to get into a business where you would like to work. You are smart and a hard worker, and you will be able to work up into a good job." Altschuler encouraged him. Then he asked, "What do you want to do, anyway?"

Dutch did not know what to answer. He really wanted to be an actor, but he couldn't bring himself to say that because it seemed so far-fetched. The only thing he could say was that he would like to be a radio announcer.

Altshuler shook his head. "I'm sorry, but that's an area I don't know anything about . . . and don't have any connections that could help you. But if that is what you want, I would suggest you get a job in radio, even if it is only sweeping the floor! That will get you in, and you can go up from there."

At the end of the summer, Dutch applied for a job at Montgomery Ward's in the sports department, but he really wanted to get a job at a radio station. He decided that he would have to try at least. So he went to Chicago to apply at the radio stations. To his disappointment, no one was interested in a young man with no experience. He received his best advice when one young lady at NBC told him to apply at smaller stations "out in the sticks." She said these smaller stations couldn't afford to compete with the big radio stations, and sometimes they would be willing to give a newcomer an opportunity.

So Dutch returned to Dixon, and found, not only had he not found a job in Chicago, George Joyce had gotten the job in the sports department at Montgomery Ward's! When he told Nelle and Jack about the advice he had received in Chicago, Jack said, "Take my car. Spend a day looking around and see what you can find."

So Dutch borrowed his father's car and set out. He drove seventy miles to the radio station he had first listened to on Howard Hall's crystal radio set, WOC in Davenport, Iowa. The station manager, a Scotsman named Peter MacArthur gave Dutch a chance to try out.

MacArthur put Dutch in a studio before a microphone and told him to announce an imaginary football game. "Tell me about a football game so that I can really see it!"

Dutch thought for only a few moments, and then he decided to describe the fourth quarter of a game between Eureka College and Western State University. He sat up straight and took a deep breath. When the red light came on in the studio he started. His heart pounded and his throat was dry, but he soon got carried away with his own

description. For twenty minutes he described every play and when he had finished, he was wet with sweat!

Based on this performance, MacArthur gave him the chance to announce the next four University of Iowa games and paid him five dollars a game and bus fare. Dutch did so well on the first game that MacArthur raised his pay to ten dollars a game and bus fare. Finally, in February 1933 he got a full-time staff announcer's job for one hundred dollars a month.

Dutch felt like he was really in the money and that he could afford to send money to Neil in college, and also help out his parents at home. Fortunately the situation with Nelle and Jack improved. After Franklin Delano Roosevelt became president, many government agencies were formed to try to overcome unemployment and the Depression. And Jack got a job in one of the government agencies in Dixon.

In April of 1933, Dutch was transferred to WOC's sister station WHO in Des Moines, which was a larger and more powerful station. Dutch had many interesting experiences in these early days of radio. One of his assignments was to broadcast the Chicago Cubs games. He covered these games, not from Wrigley Field in Chicago, but from the radio station in Des Moines! A telegraph operator at Wrigley Field would send the plays of the game in Morse code to the telegraph operator in the WHO radio station. As he received the information he would give Dutch the plays.

Then one time the telegraph wire went dead in the middle of the game, and Dutch just had to keep on talking. The Cubs were playing the St. Louis Cardinals. Bill Jurges was at the plate and Dizzy Dean was the Cards' pitcher. Dutch stalled as long as he could describing Jurges swinging the bat and getting ready for the pitch. He looked to the telegraph operator who was still shaking his head that he had no information. Dutch continued to talk describing the pitcher looking back toward the bases, and then getting his nod from the catcher. Finally Dutch shouted, "Here comes the pitch!" . . . and then . . . "it was a foul into the stands!" And then again, "Here comes the pitch!" and then "another foul." Dutch just kept using his imagination, and he kept describing foul balls until finally the wire came alive and he got the real information on the game! Dutch had reported the game for seven minutes with no information! The listeners who were hearing Dutch broadcast the game from WHO heard a very different ball game, from what had really happened! Dutch had to laugh when he got the note from the telegrapher, that Jurges had struck out on the very first pitch!"

After Neil graduated from Eureka, he visited Dutch in Des Moines and sometimes he filled in for Dutch when he was out of town for football broadcasts. This led to Moon being hired as a staff announcer at WOC, and eventually he became a program director at WOC.

Dutch really enjoyed his four years in Des Moines at WHO. He made many friends. He joined the Fourteenth Cavalry Regiment as a reserve officer, which gave him an opportunity to ride horses and also to receive training in horsemanship.

Dutch had the opportunity to interview the show people and movie stars that came to Des Moines for WHO. Among the people he interviewed were Jimmy Cagney and also a young Hollywood actress, Joy Hodges. He still wanted to be an actor himself, and he kept thinking about Hollywood.

The Cubs wintered at Catalina Island off the coast of California. Dutch talked the radio station into letting him take his vacation time to go to California to cover the Cubs' spring training. While he was in California he got in touch with Joy Hodges. She introduced him to her agent, Bill Meiklejohn, who arranged for Dutch to have a screen test at Warner Brothers. Unfortunately he had to get back to his job in Des Moines before he knew the outcome of the test. He was worried that he had spoiled his chances in Hollywood by leaving. But on March 22, 1937, he received a telegram from his agent: WARNERS OFFER CONTRACT SEVEN YEARS, ONE YEAR'S OPTION, STARTING AT $200 A WEEK. WHAT SHALL I DO?

Dutch wired back immediately: SIGN BEFORE THEY CHANGE THEIR MINDS.

Chapter Twelve

In May of 1937, Dutch quit his job at WHO, packed up his belongings, and set out for California in his sporty new Nash convertible! He felt like he was in a dream world. He thought about all the years he had sat in movie theaters watching the actors and actresses in the films from Hollywood, and now he was going to have a chance to be in the movies himself! He thought about how he had been disappointed that he hadn't gotten the job at Montgomery Ward's, then he had gotten the opportunity to be an announcer at

WOC. From that he had gotten the announcer's job at WHO in Des Moines, and now he had a contract to be an actor in the movies! He thought about how his mother always said, "Everything always turns out for the best." Dutch whistled as he drove along through the plains and desert and then on into sunny California.

The first thing that happened when he reported to Warner Brothers was that the executives decided he would have to change his name! "We can't put the name Dutch Reagan on a theater marquee," one of the men said.

Many of the stars lost their own names and were named by the studio with a name that the studio thought sounded like a movie star. They discussed what his name would be. Dutch looked around the table as they mentioned one name and then another, without paying any attention to him. He was so anxious to be in the movies, that he didn't mind if they changed his name from Dutch, however, he thought it could be his own name, Ronald Reagan. He finally got an opportunity to speak and suggested, "What about Ronald? . . . Ronald Reagan."

The executives at the table repeated his name, and finally one man spoke up and said, "I like it." And the others agreed.

In his very first picture, *Love Is on the Air,* Dutch was cast as a fast-talking radio announcer. However, before the movie went into production, the studio hairdresser gave him a new hairstyle. The wardrobe people decided that his strong swimmer's shoulders were too broad. They had shirts tailored with collars to make his neck look longer and his shoulders less broad. And then he was taught how to reach the chalk marks on the set without looking down.

Dutch was happy. He was an actor and he was in the movies! He was very easy to work with and acted in any movie he was assigned to do. That first year he was in Hollywood, he was in eight movies! These "B" movies were low budget and were turned out quickly to go to the movie theaters to appear as a second feature with the expensive "A" movies with the better-known stars.

As soon as he felt sure that he had a secure job in the movies, he sent for his mother and father to come to California. He bought a nice house for them. It was the first home they had ever owned! At that time Jack was ill with heart problems and was unable to work. He would take walks through the neighborhood, but he really wanted something useful to do. Ronald arranged for him to pick up the fan letters and send out autographed pictures, and Jack enjoyed doing this. Nelle soon found her good works through her church and also, she went to hospitals to visit the sick.

Oftentimes, on Sunday evenings, Dutch

would take his mother and father to dinner at LaRue's, a famous Hollywood restaurant. This was remarkable in Hollywood for a handsome young bachelor to go out to dinner with his parents rather than a glamorous young lady.

Moon also moved to California and many of their college friends came and Dutch helped them find jobs. Many times his friends stayed with Nelle and Jack until they could find jobs and their own apartments.

Ronald became a movie star, and was in movies with many of the big-time stars, however, he spent most of his free time with his old friends from the Midwest. They all got together for good times. They enjoyed going to the beach, riding horseback, and playing softball. Dutch usually went to church with Nelle, and often the whole group of friends would go to Nelle and Jack's for Sunday dinner after church.

Ronald Reagan became accepted in the

Warner Brothers company of actors. He appeared in films with Dick Powell, Jimmy Cagney, Errol Flynn, Pat O'Brien, Ann Sheridan, Doris Day, Wayne Morris, Eddie Albert, Humphrey Bogart, Bette Davis, Jane Wyman, Patricia Neal, Ginger Rogers, Barbara Stanwyck, and many other stars.

One director was quoted as saying Reagan was a delight to work with. He was always on time and cooperative. His excellent memory for his lines enabled him to be always well prepared even with very little preparation time.

From 1937 to 1966, Ronald Reagan appeared in fifty-three films! In several of his early films he played the part of Secret Service Agent Lieutenant Brass Bancroft. He said, "These were action pictures. . . . I fought in prisons. . . . I fought in an airplane. I swam with bullets hitting the water six inches from my face!"

In 1938, Reagan played one of three cadets in the movie, *Brother Rat*. Jane

Wyman, a pretty young actress, was also in the film.

Ronald Reagan wanted Warner Brothers to film the story of Knute Rockne, the Notre Dame football coach, so that he could play the role of George Gipp, the hero of the team. The studio decided to make the film with Pat O'Brien as Knute Rockne, but they did not want to cast Reagan as George Gipp! They said that he didn't look like a football player. Ronald went home and found a picture of himself in his college football uniform, and slammed it down on the producer's desk. He got the part!

George Gipp died in the movie, and before his death he made a final request to Knute Rockne that the team "win one for the Gipper."

The movie had its premiere at Notre Dame on October 4 and 5, 1940, when the cast went to South Bend, Indiana. In addition, Jane Wyman, Rudy Vallee, Bob Hope, and Franklin D. Roosevelt, Jr. went along, and Kate Smith, the singer, brought her weekly radio program.

Ronald Reagan and Pat O'Brien reenacted scenes from the movie before an audience in the John Adams High School, which was carried on the radio from coast to coast. Reagan recited his lines from memory and the audience was enchanted by the performance. At the end of the program, Kate Smith sang "God Bless America," with the Notre Dame choir.

Nelle had told Ronald that Jack really would like to go too. Ronald had been a little doubtful, because he was concerned that his father might have a problem with his drinking. However, he checked with the studio, and they gave their approval for Jack Reagan to go along. He made great friends with Pat O'Brien and had a wonderful time! In only about a year Jack died, and Dutch was glad that his father had that final happy experience.

Jane Wyman and Ronnie had begun dating, not too long after they had worked together in *Brother Rat*. On January 26, 1940, they were married, and after a rainy honeymoon in Palm Springs they moved into Jane Wyman's apartment in Beverly Hills. Their daughter, Maureen, was born on January 4, 1941, and they adopted their newborn son, Michael, on March 15, 1945.

Ronald was not always happy with the movies he made. Wallace Beery and Lionel Barrymore upstaged him in *The Badmen*, and he had only a supporting role in *Dark Victory* with Bette Davis, George Brent, and Humphry Bogart. He played the second lead to Errol Flynn in *Desperate Journey* and also in *Santa Fe Trail*. In *Santa Fe Trail* Reagan played Lieutenant George Custer, Olivia de Havilland was Kit Carson Halliday, and Flynn played J.E.B. Stuart.

In one scene Errol Flynn persuaded the director to place Reagan behind some other actors, who were taller than Ronald, so that he wouldn't be seen very well. The scene was a group of Confederate cavalry officers around a campfire. Dutch recognized what Flynn had done, and as they rehearsed, he kept kicking up a mound of dirt, and when the scene was shot he stood up on the mound and was easily seen over the heads of the men in front of him!

Ronald Reagan felt he reached the peak of his career with his fine performance in *King's Row* with Ann Sheridan. *King's Row* was praised by both the critics and the public, and as a result Reagan signed a new seven-year contract with Warner Brothers for a total salary of $1 million.

Ronald Reagan was very popular with his fans. In 1941, of all the Warner Brothers stars, he was second only to Errol Flynn in receiving the most fan mail!

But Reagan's movie career, along with his new contract, was interrupted with the

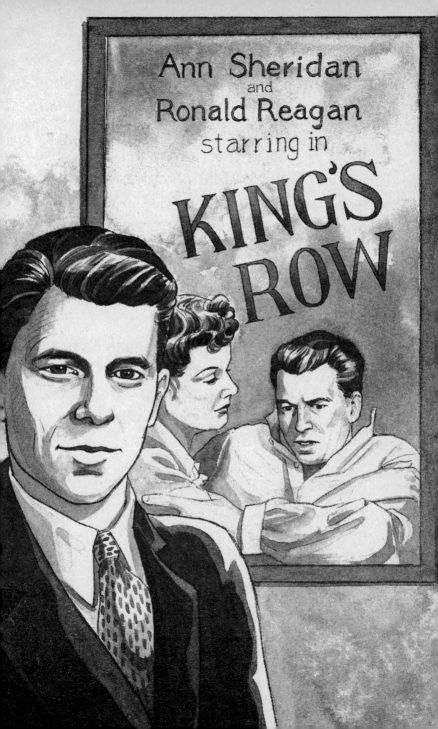

Ann Sheridan
and
Ronald Reagan
starring in

KING'S
ROW

bombing of Pearl Harbor and the declaration of war by the United States on Japan, Germany, and Italy. As a reserve officer of the U.S. Cavalry, he was called into active service. Because of his poor eyesight, Dutch was placed on limited service in the United States Army Air Corps. He spent the war years with a unit making training films for the air force in a studio, which they jokingly called Fort Roach, because before the war it was the Hal Roach Studio.

After the war Reagan returned to his movie career. He spent four months in England making *The Hasty Heart* with Patricia Neal. He made a total of twenty-two films after he was discharged from the air force, including playing a veterinarian in *Stallion Road*. He was in *Storm Warning* with Doris Day and Ginger Rogers; *The Hagen Girl* with Shirley Temple; *Bedtime with Bonzo* with Doris Day again; *The Voice of the Turtle* with Eleanor Parker, and many others.

Though Dutch continued acting in the movies, he became very active in the Screen Actors Guild. This was a union to which the movie stars and actors and actresses belonged. He was on the board of directors and was elected as president of the group in 1947.

Reagan was called to testify before the House Un-American Activities Committee investigating Communist activities along with other Hollywood stars, including his good friends, Robert Taylor, Robert Montgomery, Gary Cooper, and George Murphy. There was concern about people with alleged Communist loyalties taking over some of the unions and guilds.

Reagan was asked how do you keep Communists out of the Screen Actors Guild. Reagan replied, "The Screen Actors Guild makes democracy work by ensuring everyone a vote and by keeping everyone informed. I believe that, as Thomas Jefferson put it, if all the American people know all of the facts they will never make a mistake."

He was reelected president of the Screen Actors Guild each year until 1952. Then in 1959 he was again elected as president of the Screen Actors Guild.

During these years there were many troubling problems for the group, including strikes by some of the other unions and also the concern of how the Hollywood actors and actresses would be treated by the new television industry. With the working through of all these difficulties, which confronted the Screen Actors Guild, Ronald Reagan became very interested in the many issues that affect our nation.

Jane Wyman, meanwhile, had concentrated on improving her acting in the movies and worked on getting good acting roles. She was nominated for an Academy Award for her role in *The Yearling* and won an Oscar for her performance as a deaf mute in *Johnny*

Belinda. Jane and Ronald's interests had become very different and in 1948, Jane Wyman filed for divorce from Ronald Reagan.

These years were a very busy, difficult time for Ronald. He was trying to get good roles in the movies, and, of course, he was sad about his divorce. He had a very serious case of pneumonia and then later broke his leg while he was playing softball. However, he was very successful in his work on the problems of the Screen Actors Guild and he became recognized as a leader in the acting community.

Chapter Thirteen

During this time, Nancy Davis came into Ronald's life, and after a courtship of two years or so, they were married in March of 1952. Afterward Reagan said, "Sometimes I think my life really began when I met Nancy."

They had met when Mervyn LeRoy, a well-known director, telephoned Ronald Reagan, who was president of the Screen Actors Guild to ask him to help Nancy Davis clear up a misunderstanding about her name. It seemed there was a Nancy Davis in

Hollywood who was named as a Communist sympathizer, and Nancy wanted to clear her name that she was not this person.

Ronald made the necessary calls to clear up the problem, and made arrangements to meet Nancy Davis for dinner to talk about the situation. They liked each other so well, that they began going out together.

Nancy was a lovely young lady, who had grown up in Chicago and had graduated from Smith College, where she had majored in drama. Her mother had been an actress, and she encouraged Nancy in her career as an actress. Nancy had played in a touring company, on Broadway, and had done some television work before she came to Hollywood.

At the time of their marriage, Nancy had made eight movies and had been praised by the critics for her acting. Nancy gave up her movie career when she married Ronald, and after their marriage made only one film. She felt that her marriage was her most important career.

At this time Ronald had been in several films that he felt did not advance his career. So he decided and Nancy agreed that he would only take movie roles if they were good ones. Then his career took another turn. He was offered a role on television hosting the General Electric Theater, which was to be presented weekly. As the host, he presented the play each week and also acted in several of the plays throughout the year. During the eight years from 1954 to 1962 the GE Theater was one of the most popular drama series, ranking as one of television's top programs week after week.

In addition to the weekly television presentation, Reagan's job was expanded to include visiting General Electric factories and speaking to their employees. He met the workers and talked with them, sharing his beliefs about the country and more importantly, he listened to the concerns of the working people. In one, two-year period he visited all of General Electric's 135 plants all over the country and had personal contact with over 250,000 people! He became so popular as a speaker that he was also scheduled to talk to civic groups all over the country. He told his audiences again and again, "We are told that taxes can't be reduced until spending is cut." He said that government would always find a way to spend the money it gets. He quoted Supreme Court Justice Oliver Wendell Holmes, "Reduce taxes and spending. Keep government poor and remain free."

His speeches always included the importance of the individual and running our government for the good of all the people. Ronald Reagan was always optimistic about what a great country we have, and how bright our country's future was. The people who heard Ronald Reagan speak came away feeling good about the opportunities we have in this country.

Ronald and Nancy had become parents in 1952 with the birth of Patricia Ann and then Ronald Prescott was born in 1958. And during this time they had built a new all-electric home for their family, which was furnished with all the General Electric equipment and appliances.

After eight years the General Electric Theater went off the air, and Ronald went on to host *Death Valley Days*, another popular weekly dramatic television show. Reagan was offered this job by his brother, Neil, who was a vice president of McCann-Ericson Advertising Agency, and it was one of his accounts, U. S. Borax, which sponsored *Death Valley Days*.

Reagan was becoming more and more interested in politics and the governing of a nation. Though Jack Reagan had been a

Democrat and Ronald had been reared a Democrat, as the years went on and he developed his own thinking, he became a Republican. In 1962 he changed his party registration from Democrat to Republican. He was becoming well known for his speeches on political issues, and in 1964 he was asked to make a campaign speech on television for Barry Goldwater, the Republican candidate for president of the United States. Ronald Reagan taped a speech entitled, "A Time for the Choosing," which was played on television on October 27, 1964. Goldwater lost the election to John F. Kennedy, but there were many people who said that on the basis of his fine speech, if Reagan had been running for president, they would have voted for him!

Many important friends, including his brother, Neil, tried to persuade Ronald Reagan to run for public office. Finally he was persuaded to run for the governorship of California, and in 1966 he was elected the governor of California.

Ronald Reagan had campaigned that he would run the state of California more economically. During his first term as governor, he cut the budget for all state agencies, which was not popular. He also was very tough on the university protests, and he asked for and received the highest tax raise in California history. These were unpopular. However, at the end of his first term as governor, he had achieved some of the goals he had set for himself.

In 1970, Reagan was reelected governor of California. His management style was much like the head of a large corporation. He set goals and appointed staff to carry out the day-to-day operation to reach those goals. Though not all of his programs were popular, his eight-year governorship achieved many improvements for the state of California.

In 1976, Reagan ran for the Republican

Party presidential nomination, and lost the nomination to Gerald Ford, who, in turn, lost the election to Jimmy Carter. Reagan continued giving his speeches countrywide, and was encouraged by many important men and women to run again for the Republican nomination for president.

In 1980, Ronald Reagan won the nomination of the Republican Party as their candidate for the president of the United States and was elected by an overwhelming majority, carrying forty-four out of fifty states!

On January 21, 1981, Ronald Wilson Reagan, with his hand on his mother's well-worn Bible, took the oath of office as the fortieth president of the United States. His message to the country was one of encouragement and a call to the renewal of determination, courage, and strength to build a bright new future.

The inaugural festivities began with a fireworks display, and continued with many balls and performances by many Hollywood stars, including Frank Sinatra, Jimmy Stewart, and Johnny Carson, as they celebrated an optimistic future.

President Reagan came to Washington with his plans made for achieving that future. He appointed three men, James Baker III as chief of staff, Michael Deaver as deputy chief of staff, and Edwin Meese III, White House counselor, and delegated a great deal of responsibility to each of them in handling the details of government.

President Reagan's days fell into a routine that, for the most part, he followed for his eight years in office. (He was reelected to a second term in 1984.) His day began about seven thirty, when he breakfasted with his wife, Nancy, while they read *The New York Times,* and *The Washington Post*. The president sometimes also read some of the homework from the previous night. At a

little before nine, he took the elevator from the family quarters to the first floor of the White House and walked to the Oval Office in the West Wing.

At nine there was usually a meeting with the vice president and the top staff people to go over the business of the day and talk about any new problems, which had occurred in the past twenty-four hours. At nine thirty the national security advisor joined them, and reported on what had happened in world affairs since their last meeting. The balance of the day consisted of meetings with congressmen, world leaders, staff people, and other important people. Sometimes he was scheduled for speeches or other events.

President Reagan usually had a light lunch in the Oval Office, and once a week, on Thursday, he had a lunch meeting with Vice President George Bush. About five o'clock, he left the Oval Office and went upstairs where he changed clothes, went into the gym, and worked out with exercise equipment for a half hour and then showered.

Many times there were state dinners or other events on the calendar. But if there were no official duties planned, Ronald and Nancy had their dinners on portable tables in a small study in the family quarters, as they watched the three network news shows on tape.

After dinner he studied his paperwork and after he was done, he would retire with a book at about ten or eleven.

Ronald Reagan entered his term as president, committed to his economic plan. He planned to ask for a large cut in the taxes people pay to the government. He planned to ask that the government agencies spend less. But he planned to increase the money spent on improving and increasing the military power of the United States, which he felt, was extremely important in the cold war with the Soviet Union.

Chapter Fourteen

President Reagan spent his efforts in working with Congress and making speeches to the people so they could understand why he felt it was so important to make taxes lower and for the government to spend less money. He felt that taxes were so high that people were not able to keep enough of their own money, and he felt strongly that too much money was being spent by the government.

President Reagan thought it was extremely important that there be communication between the president and the people. So he went back to his days on radio, and he started a Saturday radio show where he talked with the people each week.

President Reagan made a very important speech in February of 1981 presenting his program for reducing taxes, cutting government spending and government controls, and following a policy on money to cut inflation. The American people agreed with the need for a new money policy, and they felt a confidence in the optimism of Ronald Reagan to accomplish his goals.

On March 30, 1981, in a Washington, D.C., hotel, President Reagan made a speech supporting his program. As he left the hotel, a young, mentally ill man opened fire on the president's group as they came out of the hotel door. Shots rang out and bullets flew in rapid succession. Secret Service Agent Tim McCarthy was hit in the chest, Patrolman Thomas Delahanty was shot in the neck, and

Press Secretary James Brady was grievously wounded.

Secret Service Agent Jerry Parr shoved President Reagan into the limo and leaped on top of him to protect him. Reagan felt terrible pain as Parr landed on him. He thought that his rib was broken! The limousine driver took off quickly to return to the White House. They had gone only a few blocks when President Reagan started to cough up bright red blood, and Parr immediately shouted to the driver, "To George Washington Hospital!" He knew that the bright red blood meant that the president's lung was punctured. The president had been shot!

Though Reagan walked to the door of the hospital, he collapsed as he went inside and it was soon clear to the emergency room doctors that his wound was critical. Nancy Reagan rushed to his side as soon as she heard of the shooting. As he saw her, he pulled off his oxygen mask and said, with his characteristic humor, "Honey, I forgot to duck!"

Nancy was terrified when she saw her husband stretched out on a gurney being prepared for surgery. His face was pale and drawn under the oxygen mask. As he was being taken to surgery, he said to the doctor, "I hope you are a Republican."

The doctor replied soberly, "Today, Mr. President, we are all Republicans."

The American people did not realize how critical President Reagan's injury was. When the surgeons removed the bullet from his chest, it was less than an inch from his heart! Despite his own pain, he was concerned about the condition of those dedicated men who had been injured with him, and was compassionate toward the young man who had inflicted such pain.

President Reagan showed his wit and grace with humor to comfort not only his family and aides but also to reassure the American people! He was truly heroic in the face of his own life being threatened.

Reagan's recovery was remarkable, given his age and the severity of his wound. Throughout his recuperation his optimism for the future gave confidence and hope to the country.

Less than a month after being shot, Reagan addressed Congress on April 28 to present his budget and tax plans. He was received with thunderous applause from Congress and the public. Despite his injury, he did his part in his fight for his budget. He met 69 times with 467 congressmen, and made innumerable phone calls during his first 100 days in office.

During his first term, Reagan was able to get Congress to pass legislation, which lowered taxes over a three-year program, and also to support cuts in the spending of the domestic government programs. Along with the accomplishment of the tax cuts, President Reagan was steadfast in his commitment to the military buildup, so that our armed forces would be second to none, and that our military equipment and weaponry would be the very best. This military superiority was the base of his strategy with the Soviet Union, and most analysts credit this military strength for the eventual collapse of the Soviet Union.

The economy of the United States slowed down from 1981 to 1983 and the national debt rose, which many people blamed on "Reaganomics," Reagan's economic policy. However, in 1984 the economic conditions improved, and Reagan said he knew it was working well, because when it became successful, no one called it "Reaganomics" any longer.

In a television address on March 23, 1983, Reagan announced the beginning of work on a new defense program, the Strategic

Defense Initiative, or as it was popularly called "Star Wars." The purpose of Star Wars was to provide a protective shield against nuclear attack. Many critics made fun of Star Wars, and others said they thought this might lead to a new phase in the cold war and risk a nuclear strike before the protective shield could be built.

As it turned out, the critics were wrong, and as Margaret Thatcher, the prime minister of England said later, "President Reagan's Strategic Defence Initiative . . . was to prove central to the West's victory in the Cold War. Looking back it is now clear to me that Reagan's original decision on SDI was the single most important of his presidency."

The prospect of the United States developing such a protective shield was a very influential step in bringing the end to the cold war with the Soviet Union. President Reagan was constant in his distrust of the

Communist system, and called the cold war between the United States and the Soviet Union a "struggle between right and wrong and good and evil," despite criticism from those who felt he was dangerously close to provoking war with Russia.

Chapter Fifteen

In 1984, Ronald Reagan was reelected president of the United States by a landslide vote, carrying forty-nine states! He lost only in Minnesota, the home state of his opponent Walter F. Mondale, and the District of Columbia. As he greeted his supporters on election night, he listed some of the accomplishments of his first term: lower inflation, more jobs, cuts in federal spending, and strengthened military forces, but he ended saying, "Our work isn't finished."

President Reagan went to the Oval Office

each day and met with his advisors. His style was to allow his staff the authority to make decisions within his or her area of responsibility. He was always friendly and respectful, and he always saw the best in everyone. He loved to tell stories and had a keen sense of humor. In many of his stories he would make fun of himself.

The most enduring quality of President Reagan's entire life is his optimism. He always had the conviction that everything turns out for the best, and he had the ability to give that assurance to others that everything is going to be all right.

He had dignity and had a great respect for the office of the presidency. He always dressed in a suit and tie when he was in the Oval Office. He did not remove his suit jacket, nor did he wear casual clothes during his workday in the Oval Office.

He and Nancy enjoyed their weekends at Camp David, where they could be casual, and often enjoyed watching old movies in the evening there. He loved going to his ranch in California, Rancho del Cielo, his ranch in the sky. When he was there he wore jeans and a cowboy hat. He would cut brush or sometimes split logs. Most of all he liked to ride horseback. The Secret Service men had trouble keeping up with him as he rode and jumped the fences.

Ronald Reagan was a man who considered himself to be a citizen-politician, a man just like all the other citizens of this great United States. Many of his biographers consider his greatest strength that he could identify with the people of this country, and his extraordinary ability in communicating with his fellow citizens. Reagan's skill in speaking to the public was superb. He said that when he made a speech he didn't talk to the crowds of people. He talked to people on a personal basis, just as if he were talking to friends in his own living room or in the barbershop.

He never thought he was better than other people. As president he was still writing letters to his friends that he had been writing to for fifty years. He received thousands of letters from children, people with problems, and old people. The mail service in the White House would send him fifty or so letters a week, which he would answer personally, and he would often send money to strangers and friends. One time he sent a check for a hundred dollars to a woman who wouldn't cash it, because the signature of Ronald Reagan on the check was worth more than the hundred dollars of the check. Reagan called the bank to give her the money, and sent her his signature, which she could keep.

President Reagan showed great compassion for victims of tragedy. On December 16, 1985, he and Mrs. Reagan gave comfort to the families of the 248 servicemen on their way home for the holidays, who were killed in the plane crash in Gander, Newfoundland.

And then, only a few short weeks later in January 1986, the explosion of the spaceship *Challenger*, killing all the seven astronauts on board, devastated the nation. President and Mrs. Reagan grieved with the families of the astronauts. President Reagan spoke to the country, stressing the future, and honoring the astronauts, as he quoted that the seven *Challenger* astronauts had "slipped the surly bonds of earth to touch the face of God."

In 1985, with America strong both economically and militarily, Reagan felt the time had come for the leaders of the two countries, the United States and the Soviet Union, to meet. Mikhail Gorbachev agreed to meet Reagan in Geneva in November.

As Gorbachev, in his awkward bulky coat, heavy scarf and hat, got out of his limousine, President Ronald Reagan in his well-tailored blue suit walked briskly to meet him at the foot of the stairs. Calmly and with supreme self-confidence, President Reagan greeted Gorbachev.

Reagan and Gorbachev developed a respect and liking for each other, though not much was accomplished at this meeting. Reagan had come to the meeting to get the Soviet Union to reduce nuclear weapons, and Gorbachev had come to get Reagan to abandon Star Wars.

There were two more meetings, the one at Reykjavik, Iceland, where Gorbachev would not negotiate unless the United States abandoned Star Wars. Reagan absolutely refused and walked out! At the time, many of the critics were aghast, but later it was clear that the conference at Reykjavik was the turning point in the treaties, which brought the cold war to an end.

Along with the accomplishments of the economic recovery in the United States and the end of the cold war, unfortunately President Reagan had to deal with the Iran-Contra scandal. With his enthusiasm for assisting the Contras and his deep concern for the release of the hostages in Iran, some of the officials in his administration, using their own judgment, thought they were doing what President Reagan would want them to do. The stress was high within the White House, and finally a saddened President Reagan made a statement accepting the responsibility for the selling of arms to Iran in exchange for the release of the hostages, though he had not felt that was what had been done. The other part of the picture, that some of that money had been used for the Contras had been beyond his knowledge.

In December of 1987, Gorbachev came to Washington for the third summit meeting to sign the INF treaty, which eliminated all Soviet SS-20 and NATO Pershing II intermediate range missiles in Europe. This was part of Reagan's offer, which the Soviets had rejected at Reykjavik, and now Gorbachev agreed to Reagan's terms, Star Wars and all!

Reagan then went to Moscow for a fourth summit at Gorbachev's invitation, where he continued to push for the pursuit of freedom. A year before, in his visit to Berlin, Reagan had stood at the Brandenburg Gate at the Berlin Wall, and said, "Mr. Gorbachev, open this gate! Mr. Gorbachev, tear down this wall!"

In November 1989 the Berlin Wall came tumbling down. In 1989 the Soviet Union pulled out of Afghanistan. In 1989, Lech Walesa, the head of the Polish Labor Party with years of protest against the Soviet Union, was elected president of Poland. The other countries of Eastern Europe gained their independence and finally the rest of the Soviet Union came apart! On Christmas Day of 1991 the Soviet Union was dissolved!

The economic and military policies of President Ronald Reagan were critical contributions to the end of the cold war and to the fall of the Soviet Union. History will make the final judgment.

President Ronald Reagan wrote his last letter to his country in 1994, when he revealed that he had been diagnosed with Alzheimer's disease, and he said, " . . . in closing let me thank you, the American people, for giving me the great honor of allowing me to serve as your President. When the Lord calls me home, whenever that may be, I will leave with the greatest love for this country of ours and eternal optimism for its future."

Acknowledgments

I would like to acknowledge my appreciation to Marilyn Jones of the Ronald Reagan Boyhood Home Museum; Bob Gibler and Stella Grobe of the Lee County Historical Society; Lloyd and Amy McElhiney of the Ronald Reagan Birthplace Museum; Mrs. Bess Reagan; Mrs. Helen Lawton; Dr. Lamar Wells; Mrs. Ruth Walters; Dixon Chamber of Commerce; Dixon Public Library; University of California at Los Angeles Oral History Program; The Office of President Reagan; The Ronald Reagan Presidential Library; The Downers Grove Public Library and the Interlibrary Loan System as well as the resources of the Internet.